A Horse With Wings

By

Julie Atwood

Copyright © 2010 julie atwood
First Edition

All Rights Reserved. No part of this book may be reproduced in any manner whatsoever without written permission of the author, except in the case of brief quotations in articles and reviews. The author may be contacted by email at mjlr_books@mjlr.com.

For additional copies of this book, goto http://www.createspace.com/3472437.

Printed in the United States of America
ISBN 1453726608
EAN-13 9781453726600

DEDICATION

This book has been a family project, put together for me in love. I dedicate it to my wonderful husband and my two precious daughters, who prayed for me and did everything for me except the actual writing. (They decided to leave that part to me!)

1. A HORSE WITH WINGS..................................1
2. SOMETHING ELSE AGAIN 7
3. A TWO-EYED FRIEND 13
4. A NOT-REALLY GROWN-UP 21
5. MAKING THINGS UP 29
6. THE SECRET OF HAVE AND BRAVE.......... 35
7. KIDNEY GARDEN 43
8. WORRIED 51
9. OBSERVING 57
10. SONIA 63
11. THE LION INSIDE ME............................... 69
12. A DIFFERENT KIND OF COURAGE.......... 77
13. TUTORS AND GENIUSES......................... 81
14. A NOBLE DEED 89
15. CHANGES 97
16. STINK BOMBS AND SNOWFLAKES 103
17. FIRST PLACE WINNERS 107
18. STORKS AND BABIES 115

19. ALONE	123
20. TWO BABIES AND A MAN	133
21. WASHING KITTY CLEAN	141
22. DIRTY	151
23. GETTING SAVED TWO WAYS	159
24. TWO BIRTHDAY PARTIES	165
25. STILL GOOD FRIENDS	173
26. GROWING UP TWO WAYS	181
27. PEGASUS WRITES HER PUBLISHER	189
AUTHOR'S NOTE	191

1.

A HORSE WITH WINGS

My realife name is Margaret Elizabeth Kendall. I am five fingers old. Daddy explained me fingers really means years. I am not sure what is the difference between years and fingers, but cept I think years are lots bigger and shaped round like wheels. Plus, there are 1983 of those years. I know, cause that's what it says on our kitchen calendar. And 1983 are too many years for me to count.

Fingers are lots easier to count. I got five fingers on one of my two hands and five fingers on the other hand. Alan, my second-grade brother, told me that makes ten. I can count to ten. Alan keeps ten earthworms in the bug box under his bed.

Fingers look like earthworms, long and pink and squiggly. But they stay sticked on tight to your hands the same way Motorthroat's tail stays sticked onto her kitty bottom. If you pulled them off, it would hurt. Fingers can be anything you tell them to be, like churches or steeples or peoples. But never point them at a grown-up, or Mommy will get mad.

Mommy's fingers can tie my shoestrings into bows. My friend Haley can tie bows with her own fingers. But my fingers just act stubborn, mixing up the strings into tangled spaghettis. When they do this, I make them give each other a good spanking.

Mommy spanks me sometimes for being rude to Mrs. Winthrop, the lady who lives next door. Mrs. Winthrop gots scrambled egg hair and a fat brown bug on her nose that never jumps off. She likes to say, in a voice like rusty frog, "Children should be seen and not heard."

But she asks me silly questions that I got to answer anyways. And her kisses make spit all over my face.

This morning when I run into the living room, there sits Mrs. Winthrop in the fat green chair. She stares at me through her dead-fish eyes, smiling her pretend smile. "Really, Peggy dear," she says in her froggy voice. "A young lady shouldn't run through the house like that. Now come over here and give me a kiss, Peggy."

"I am not a peggy," I tell her, walking backwards. "Peggies are those little round sticks we hang our jackets on."

"Really!" Her eyebrows jump up into the scrambled eggs. "Now surely a big girl like you must know that Peggy is short for Margaret."

"Is not!" I argue. "That's just silly, they don't even sound the same. *Peggy* is short for . . ." I stop and think a minute. Then I remember my favorite story Daddy reads me at bedtime. "Pegasus," I finish. "He is a horse with wings."

"Nonsense." Mrs. Winthrop's face puffs up like Alan's bullfrog when someone pokes him with a stick. She looks so funny I laugh.

I say, "You gots a big brown bug on your nose."

Just then Mommy storms into the living room. She must have heard me say that, cause she grabs my arms and shakes me so hard my teeth feel dizzy. Then she plops down on a chair and whomps me upside-down over her legs, and she spanks my bottom. Hard. Three times. "Margaret Elizabeth Kendall," she says between her teeth. "That was rude. Go to your room at once."

Upstairs in my room I throw my pillow on the rug. I stomp it with both my feets. The pillow is Mrs. Winthrop first, and then she turn into Mommy. At last she's just my pillow again, soggy and wet from my crying.

Crying makes the mad lion jump out my tummy and swim away on my tears. Then I feel empty and sad inside until my mommy comes.

She always comes at just that time.

Mommy scoops me up onto her lap when she plops down on the bed. "Margaret Elizabeth," she says, pushing back my hairs like wet strings from my forehead. She sounds like a soft wind. She shakes her head at me, but she is smiling now. "Whatever are we going to do with you?"

"I don't know." I try not to think about lions she could find to eat me. "Turn me into a nose bug?"

Mommy laughs. "Baby, you're the giddy limit," she says. "No, I think I've punished you enough. Besides, you're already something too special." She brushes my hairs with her hands and explains me about my name. Margaret means a pearl. Elizabeth means a gift from God. "The second one I don't doubt," she tells me, smiling. "But sometimes I wonder if what God gave us is—well, something precious as a pearl, of course, but just a little more—unusual."

Mommy says this to herself, but I know she's talking about me. I think of something. "Mommy! Maybe what God gave you is—a horse with wings?"

"A what?"

"A horse with wings," I say again."You know, like in Daddy's book 'bout Greek mistology."

"Mythology," Mommy corrects me. She pulls on her thinking face. "You mean Pegasus, baby?"

"Yes!" I start feeling sparkly inside. "Maybe I am really Pegasus too. Couldn't you call me that anyways? Then when Mrs. Winthrop calls me Peggy, she will not be silly."

"We'll see." Mommy shakes her head at me, but she's still smiling. "Now, about poor Mrs. Winthrop . . ."

She turns all stony-faced. "You musn't make personal remarks, because they hurt people's feelings," she explains. "Mrs. Winthrop can't help having a *wart—not* a bug—on her nose, any more than you can help having your daddy's red hair."

"I don't got Daddy's red hair," I argue. "It's orange. And plus, he taked it all with him to the Writer's Conference this weekend."

Mommy laughs again. "Poor Mrs. Winthrop," she says, wiping her eyes with her fingers. "She doesn't know what she's missing."

"What's she missing, Mommy?"

"Never mind, baby. You'll know when you're older." Mommy's face turns cloudy, with sad eyes. "Now I want you to run back downstairs and tell Mrs. Winthrop you're sorry. Okay?"

"Okay, Mommy."

I don't run. I just rake the rug with my feets. But back down in the living room, I notice Mrs. Winthrop's face looks wrinkly and saggy-sad. It sags so sad I really do feel sorry. "I'm sorry I hurt your nose's feelings," I tell her kindly. "And I'm also sorry you don't know what you're missing."

Her fish eyes shine like questions. But she doesn't ask those questions. "That's quite all right, dear," she says instead. "I don't understand children very well, never having had any of my own. But you're a good girl, I'm sure." Suddenly her wrinkles flip up into smiles. "You don't have to kiss me, Margaret. Not unless you want to."

"It's okay, Mrs. Winthrop." And I kiss her anyways.

She kisses me too, and like always I feel spit on my face. But this time I don't wipe it off till I run back out the room.

That night when Daddy comes home from his Writer's Conference, he and Mommy both laugh hard together. Their laughing sounds like lions and birds, mixed up together in the same song. And when they hug each other, their song pulls me in to be a part of the hugging.

Daddy feels scratchier than Mommy. But his smile looks the same, and his hairs got scraped from carrots same as mine. "Hey there, Pegasus!" he shouts, lifting me high to the ceiling.

I feel sparkly inside.

"Really, Daddy?" I ask hopefully. "Is that my name now?"

"Well, let's just say it's your special pretend name. Okay?"

"Okay, Daddy."

He lowers me to the floor. "Off with you now, to find Alan, Caitlin, and any other young scamps of mine."

I skip to the kitchen, where my brother and sister always do their homework on the big speckledy table. I don't know where to find any other young scamps. "Pegasus is my pretend name," I sing as I skip. "My realife name is not a peg, it's Margaret Elizabeth Kendall."

But even so, I think I feel some wings. They spring out from my back between those two pointy bones—soft as a wind, pink as fingers, and painted with lions and birds.

2.

SOMETHING ELSE AGAIN

Alan gots a realife bird. She's only dead and brown, with shiny gray marbles for eyes. He found her in the alley behind our backyard fence. When he first carried her home, he hid her in his top drawer underneath some socks. The bird made all his socks stink like spinach.

Mommy yelled, "You throw that putrid thing out at once, Alan Ray!" But he didn't. Instead, he taked the bird to school. His teacher cut her open and pulled out all the dead bird parts. Then she stuffed in little curly woods.

Now Alan's bird stands up on his windowsill, right next to his rock collection. She doesn't stink anymore, but she doesn't sing either. This is cause she's dead. Alan explained me about dead. He named his bird Pluto, but her real name is brown woodthrush. Pluto is a planet, the last one in our solar system. He explained me about planets too. I mean Alan did, not the planet Pluto who can't talk.

Alan lets me touch Pluto, and I am the only one. I mean I am the only one he lets touch his bird named Pluto. The planet Pluto is too far away for even my daddy to touch.

Besides Pluto, Alan gots one lizard, two garter snakes, three guinea pigs, four frogs, eight fishes, ten earthworms, and about a zillion bugs. I only got Motorthroat. She is a fat gray kitty with crookedy Band-Aid stripes. I named her Motorthroat cause she rumbles inside her throat the way our car does when Mommy or Daddy turns its key. They call that sound the motor, but for my kitty they say purr.

Motorthroat likes Mommy, Daddy, Caitlin, tuna, mushrooms, backrubs, chocolate chip cookies, and me when I don't wrap ribbons round her tail. When I do this, she spins round in a circle and spanks me on my nose. She spanks Alan too. She's been mad at him since yesterday, when he squirted her with the hose for chasing his favorite snake.

Alan is my favorite people, next to Daddy and Mommy. He knows all about animals, rocks, planets, bugs, numbers, computers, and a thing at school called science. I know only one thing better than him. But that is my special secret.

Alan is taller than me but littler than Caitlin. He gots twisty licorice hair and eyes like rainy leaves and a smile like a secret just for me. He never bosses me or yells at me or makes me go away when I want to ask some questions. Alan loves to answer questions. But Caitlin always says they try her soul.

Caitlin won't explain me what that means. That old Caitlin won't explain a thing. She is taller than me and Alan, miles tall but not as tall as Mommy. Her front hairs make steps instead of strings on both sides of her face, and the skins above her eyes are painted blue. She talks always on the phone to her friends in the eighth grade. Boys are all she talks about. And piano is the only thing she plays.

The piano stands in our living room, smack between the blue front window and the fat green chair. It is a long brown box with teeth. When everybody's fingers but cept mine poke the teeth, dancing songs jump out. That is called playing the piano. It is something else you're sposed to do with your fingers. Once Mommy spanked me when I played it with my feets.

My fingers don't make dancing songs. Only crookedy yells jump out the teeth, yells like lions or birds.

Lions live in the piano's window end, and birds live in the green chair end. I am not sure where live the dancing songs, maybe in the middle. But I never can poke them out by myself. Mommy tells me that's cause I need to first take piano lessons, like Alan and Caitlin gots. "When can I take them, Mommy?" I ask.

She says, "Wait till you've had a year of kidney garden first."

The kidney garden is at school, the one where Alan goes. I won't go there till the fall. I think I will like school, cause it is stories and science and secrets the big kids talk about. But that kidney garden sounds like Something Else Again.

I know what kidneys are, those long red beans that Mommy sticks in our chili. And I know about gardens too, cause Daddy digged one in our backyard. It's filled with vegetables—spinach and call flowers and, worst of all, those bumpy little trees called broccolis that stink like when you've just used the bathroom. I hope the kidney garden will smell like chili instead.

Mommy makes me eat those vegetables, everything on my plate. When she gets mad she makes by spanking. But when she feels happy she turns them into animals. "Catch that baby octopus," she calls. "Look, baby, there's a koala bear hiding behind that horse. Chase them into the cave."

So I chase them, but the cave is really my mouth and soon those vegetables are gone. I like animals better than spankings. I like them better than vegetables, too. Elephants taste better than call flowers, and giraffes taste better than those bumpy, stinky little trees.

Mommy is a big tree. Every morning, with her long hot stick that purrs, she turns her straight brown string-hairs into curly leaves. Sometimes like Caitlin she paints her eyeskins blue, but only when a night comes that she goes away with Daddy.

Mommy gots three voices—mad, funny, and happy. Her mad voice is a spanking hand. Her funny voice is laughing silver birds. And her happy voice is a soft wind swimming through the trees outside my window. I like her happy voice the best. It feels like when she rocks me in her arms.

I wish she would rock me every night like she did when I was three fingers old. But usually now she is too busy—from cooking, pick-upping things, and typing front of her little green TV that is called a computer.

Mommy and Alan like to type numbers on the computer. Caitlin likes better the TV with color pictures. But Daddy and me like books the best. Daddy gives me ones he wrote all by himself. They are filled with wishes and dreams, in words instead of pictures. "Oh, James," Mommy always says. "Aren't those books a little too old for her?"

"They are not too old," I argue. "They are brand-new books. Daddy said he just got them published."

Then Mommy and Daddy both laugh. But Daddy says nothing, he only smiles and winks at me. I wonder: Does he know my special secret?

Daddy knows lots of things, even more than Alan. But he explains us them in words too long for sitting still enough. I like better when he plays with us, a big orange laughing lion. I like best when he lifts me to the sky . . . or reads me my favorite story about that horse with wings. He calls *me* Pegasus, too. And when mad, he spanks me only with his eyes.

Daddy and Alan are slow and quiet. Mommy and Caitlin are quick and sparkly. Motorthroat is That Darn Cat, and Alan's pets are Just Impossible.

I am Something Else Again.

"What is it?" I always ask whoever says that thing.

But they never will answer me. They only shake their heads and burst out laughing.

3.

A TWO-EYED FRIEND

"Caitlin, what is a four-eyed nerd?"

Caitlin doesn't answer me. She's hunched over the piano, practicing her scales. These are piano sounds, like fingers climbing up and down some steps. Scales are also sticked onto the skins of Alan's fishes. And Mommy's scale lives in the bathroom. Whenever she stands on it, she groans. Whenever I ask questions, Caitlin also groans.

Caitlin groans right now.

"A four-eyed nerd," I say again. "Like what you told the telephone Peter Jenkins is."

Caitlin stops playing scales. She rolls her fingers into stones and spins around on her stool. Her eyes scrinch up at me, but they really look mad at something else. "Peter Jenkins," she tells me, all tight between her teeth, "is the dorkiest boy in the whole middle school."

"Does he really got four eyes?" I shut my eyes and think about this. "Are they all sticked onto his face? Or are some eyes on his knees or his tummy or his fingers?" I think some more and shiver. "If your fingers had eyes and played the piano, wouldn't they get dizzy?"

"Gross!" Caitlin yells. She bangs the piano teeth hard with both her hands. I jump when the lions roar in there, open my eyes. Caitlin's eyes shoot darts at me. "Questions, questions! Aargh, I can't *stand* it!" She shakes a finger at me. "You are a little pest, a number-one pest. Pegasus the Pest."

"I am not a pest," I argue. "Pests are insects. Insects are bugs. That's what Alan said."

"You and Alan are both pests," Caitlin tells me. "I don't know which one of you two is worse—you with your space-case questions, or Alan with his stinking old dead birds."

"Pluto doesn't stink. Ms. Hinkle cut her open and taked out all the rotten parts. Now she's stuffed with only—"

"That does it." Caitlin bangs the piano again. Tomato juice swims over her face. "Margaret Elizabeth Kendall," she says between her teeth. "I. Am. Going. To. *Murder* you! So beat it before I count to three."

I don't beat it. I just stand there and smile when Caitlin grabs her book, her one called *Intermediate Piano Method, Part B.* She throws the book at me. I duck and it bounces off the window. It's a soft book, so the window doesn't break. "Ha-ha, missed!" I laugh. "I hope you get eyes on your fingers."

Caitlin jumps up. She jumps so fast her stool bangs over on its side. She takes one step toward me, her tomato juice face turning to grape. She takes another step. I almost scream, but then the doorbell dings.

Caitlin freezes into a statue.

The doorbell dings again.

I turn me into a purple cloud, go floating down the hall. "Wait, Pegasus!" Caitlin calls, just as I reach the front door. "If that's Peter Jenkins, tell him I'm not home."

"Why?" I yell back, but only some scales answer me.

I open the door, and there stands a Caitlin-sized boy. He's frowning down at the porch and washing his hands without soap. He gots pink oatmeal skin and glasses like square windows on his eyes. There are only two of those eyes, one behind each window.

"Hello," I say, smiling. "Did you come to see Caitlin?"

He jumps backwards and stares at me. "Yes, please," he says, with some wind in his voice. "Is she here?"

"Yes, but 'cept not if you're Peter Jenkins. Then she's just practicing her scales. But don't worry, you're prob'ly somebody else."

The boy's two eyes turn into questions. He says, "I am Peter Jenkins."

"But you only got two eyes. Do you keep other eyes on your knees?"

"What eyes? What knees?" His whole face looks like a question now. "What are you talking about?"

"Your other eyes, on your regular knees," I explain. "Caitlin said you got four of those eyes. She said you are a four-eyed nerd."

Peter Jenkins sags like an opened-up balloon. Milk swims over his oatmeal face. He looks the way I feel when someone says I am too little. "Caitlin said that?"

"Yes, but that's okay. She is a yelling monster with blue skins on top her eyes, and she's always calling me a pest. I am not a pest, I am a horse with wings. But 'cept today I turned into a purple cloud."

Peter isn't listening. "I got to go," he says softly to the porch. He rakes his feets across there without picking them up. He looks so saggy-sad I want to cry.

Peter really does cry. He drops down on the top porch step and sobs into his hands. I slip outside to listen, cause I never heard a big boy cry before. It sounds interesting, like bird-squeaks and lion-growls at the same time. But it also sounds real sad, so I plunk down next to him and pet his back the way I pet my kitty. His back shakes like Jell-O, only hard and with a bone inside.

The frontyard elm tree shakes some leaves. Alan jumps from its highest branch and plops down on his tummy in the grass. He bounces back up and stares across at us. Then he darts up to the porch, smiling, flapping both his arms. "Peter! Peter!" He calls with all excited.

Alan almost never gets excited. I know then Peter must be someone special.

Peter looks up from his hands and smiles back at Alan. His tears have dried to face-stripes and to window-polka dots. "Hey, Einstein," he says, with a frog in his voice.

Alan doesn't say he isn't Einstein. He just sits down on Peter's other side and leans across to me. "Hey, Pegasus," he says, in his most sparkly voice. "You know what? Peter's in the eighth grade Science Club. He's the president!"

"Was," Peter corrects him. "School's out for the summer, remember?"

I ask, "Did you get voted president on TV?"

"No way." He grins at me, then shakes his head with cloudy eyes. "Didn't get voted at all, 'cause I was the only one who ran for office. I'm not exactly the famous type, I'm afraid."

"Don't be afraid," I comfort him. "We like you, Peter. Don't we, Alan?"

"We sure do." Alan nods. "Peter, would you please take us over to see Dileth? Will you show us how he learned to run his maze?"

"Well . . ." Peter frowns a long time, like he's thinking hard. He snuffs his nose some more. Then he blows it into his hands and wipes them on the top step. Caitlin pretends to barf when I do that.

"Please, Peter?" Alan begs.

I ask, "Who is Dileth?"

"Okay," Peter says at last, unfolding himself real slow then standing up. "Let's go, Einstein. You too, Pegasus." He smiles down at me, then answers my question. "You'll see. I think you'll like Dileth."

A TWO-EYED FRIEND

Peter's house lives only two blocks away. It looks white and woody like our house, but with tangly plants hugging its sides and crookedy wires sticking out the roof. Inside is filled with lots more plants and wires, tangled with books all over the couch and chairs. The mommy is not there. "She's at the lab with my dad," Peter explains. "They are both scientists. That's what I want to be, too."

"Me too," says Alan.

"Me three." I spin round in a circle. "A scientist who writes stories and is also a horse with wings."

Peter and Alan both laugh. But they don't do it mean the way Caitlin's boyfriend does.

Peter's room has not a bed, only a sleeping bag full of jars with bugs in them. It looks like Alan's room, only more. It smells like Alan's guinea pigs. Over in one corner sits a big brown woody box. Peter lets us look inside. The box is filled with little doors, zigging in and out like in a painting Daddy gots called Modern Art. Between two doors sits a marshmallow with fur. "That's Dileth," Peter says, pointing to the marshmallow.

Dileth blinks up at us with pink candy eyes. He gots a mousy face and an earthworm for a tail. He stands up on his people legs, shakes his tiny people hands. I ask, "Can I hold him, please?"

"Sure," Peter says. "But first let's watch him run his maze and finish with his supper."

Dileth eats leaves for supper, leaves chopped up and soggy in a cup sticked on the box. He doesn't play animals to eat them. Instead, he runs with little squeaks in and out each door. At Peter's end he cleans his cup, and then he squeaks for more. I don't think Mommy would ever spank Dileth.

Peter lets me hold him. Dileth tickles my hands, but I don't let him fall. I don't like to fall either. When I'm on the jungle gym, my best friend Haley-paley calls me a scaredy-cat. Dileth is a white rat. The box is a maze, and they are both a science project. I know, cause Peter explains all this while I am petting Dileth. I say, "Caitlin does those only for school. Now is still the summer."

"I like to learn things all the time," Peter tells us. "Even in the summer."

"Me too," Alan says.

"Me three." I scratch behind Dileth's mousy ears. "I like to learn about Dileth."

"Yes, please!" Alan grins up at Peter. "Tell us exactly how you taught him. Which method did you use?"

Peter explains which method. But he explains it same as Daddy, with words about a million miles long. So only Alan listens. I listen to Dileth instead, while he tells me in rat language how it feels to have around him giant peoples. He gets tired same as me of being the littlest one.

"You kids are great," Peter says when we are done. "I'm so happy you guys came over! But I wish..." His face turns cloudy again. "I sure wish Caitlin liked me too. I wanted her to help me with my project."

"I'll help you," Alan says. "Caitlin's not logical."

"She's silly," I add. "She hates rats and mouses. Whenever she sees them, she screams and jumps on chairs."

"I didn't mean for her to help me with Dileth. I thought maybe she could help me with the reading and writing part. You see..." Peter stops a minute. Tomato juice swims over his neck, and he stares down at his rug. "I don't read or write very good."

"Me either," Alan says, smiling and shaking his head.

My mouth opens up all by itself. I feel sparkly inside. But then I close that mouth with two clapping hands. "Remember," I remind it then, whispering. "That is s'posed to be a secret."

Peter and Alan both look at me with questions in their eyes. "What's a secret, Pegasus?" Alan sounds real curious.

"Nothing," I say quick. "But you know what? I know why Caitlin doesn't like Peter. It's 'cause he's sized like us."

"But I'm years older than you two," Peter says, looking puzzled. "I'm sized like Caitlin."

"That's only on your outside," I explain. "Anyways, I like you, Peter—even if you don't got other eyes on your knees. I wish *you* were our sister, 'stead of Caitlin."

Peter and Alan both burst out laughing.

"Peter would be our brother, not our sister," Alan explains on our way home. "Even so," he says, frowning and sucking on a stem from Dileth's leaves, "I think I understand what you meant, Pegasus."

We smile at each other. Then we turn into squeaking rats and race each other home.

4.

A NOT-REALLY GROWN-UP

Everyone big is going gone tonight.

Caitlin is going to a movie with her boyfriend Barry Bruner. (I heard her say that to the telephone.) He is furry like a bear, a growly not a friendly one. He smiles same as Jaws the Shark in the movie they're seeing, and he snarls at us like the Big Bad Wolf in my book of fairy tales. Me and Alan call him Hairy Barry. Mommy and Daddy say he is Too Old.

"They think I'm going to study at the library with that dorky Peter Jenkins," Caitlin whispers to me. "They actually like that nerd! Pegasus, please don't tell Mommy or Daddy what you heard about me and Barry. Okay? Promise not to tell if I take you and Alan next week to see *E.T.?* I just don't want them to worry—especially on their big night."

I think about this. E.T.'s one of my favorite other-planet peoples, but me and Alan saw his movie only last week. Mommy and Daddy taked us.

"Okay, Caitlin, I promise not to tell them," I say at last. "But only 'cause I don't want them to worry too."

Tonight Mommy and Daddy look too happy to feel worried. They are going gone with each other, for their anniversary. Only me and Alan have to stay home. And a baby-sitter has to come and stay here with us.

"Call Peter to come sit us," we take turns begging Caitlin.

"Certainly not." Caitlin stares at us like we got eyes on our tummies. "You guys want me to blow my cover?"

"What cover?" I ask her. "Does that mean the same as blow your stack?"

Caitlin doesn't answer me, of course. She just calls her friend Brandi to come stay with us instead.

Brandi looks like Caitlin, but with green stuff stead of blue on top her eyes. And the hairs in front her face that look like steps instead of strings are colored sand, not mud like Caitlin's hair-steps. That is the only difference.

Brandi drags herself into the living room, thunks down hard in the fat green chair. A mad and tired wind poofs out her cheeks. She bounces her hair-steps, then stares at us with nails in her eyes. They say, *What a drag, taking care of little kids!* Her mouth says, "So it's Alan and Peggy, huh?"

"No," I tell her, staring back. "I am not a peggy. I am Margaret Elizabeth Kendall."

Brandi snorts like a horse that gots no wings. "I'm not calling any little kid a thing like that. Those are old-fogey names. Maybe they're okay for that old bag who lives next door to you."

"She is a lady, not a bag. And her name is Ethel Winthrop."

"Same thing." Brandi snorts again.

"I don't think so," Alan says. "They don't sound the same. I don't read so good, but I can tell the difference between them. It's obvious."

"Oh, you little twirps are hopeless!" Brandi groans like Caitlin does and jumps out the green chair. "I'm going for a Coke."

"What do you think of her?" Alan asks me when she's gone to the kitchen.

"Hopeless!" I groan a Caitlin-Brandi groan. We giggle.

"We got to sneak away from her," Alan whispers. "But where?"

I think a minute. "I know," I whisper back to him. "We can go next door to visit Mrs. Winthrop."

"But that's not logical, Pegasus. She is hopeless too."

"I'm not sure. Brandi doesn't like her, right? So she must be cool in some way."

Alan frowns a long time. "Yes," he says at last, smiling all sparkly at me. "That is logical, Pegasus."

Brandi sends us straight to bed. "Okay," we say politely, though we got another hour. We surprise her, but she doesn't follow us upstairs. Instead, she talks on the telephone until the doorbell dings. Then she runs to answer it and lets in a bunch of her-sized boys.

Me and Alan listen from top the stairs. "She'll never notice now," I whisper, grinning. "Let's do it, okay?"

We dress ourselves in our Sunday School clothes. I pull on my strappy white shoes and my cloudy pink dress with tulips on the front. Alan zips me up the back and ties my shiny sash. He wears his itchy black suit and fixes his own necktie. But he ties it the same way he ties my sash. Only Mommy can fix it the other way.

"Let's bring her some presents," I tell him.

"Okay." Alan pulls his bug box out from under his bed. "I've got a cool June bug in here. Or would she rather have a baby garter snake?"

I shake my head. "I don't think old ladies like snakes very much. You better bring her a pretty rock instead." So Alan picks a blue one with rings round it like the planet Saturn. I tear three shiny plastic daisies off the front flap on my purse. "These kind don't need water," I explain. "Ready, Alan?"

"Yes." Alan waves his pencil flashlight for seeing in the dark outside. Then he clips it on his necktie, and we tiptoe down the stairs.

Caitlin-music booms from the living room stereo. It sounds like a chainy fence, if the fence could scream. The living room looks filled with Caitlin-sized peoples, all talking and laughing and jumping up and down. All the girls wear those funny hair-steps front their faces. Almost all the boys got hairs like rows of triangles, poking up from their heads like the ones on dinosaurs.

One boy looks bald but cept for a giant toothbrush, lying upside-down across the middle of his head. When I see him, I have to burst out laughing. But nobody hears me. And nobody even notices when me and Alan sneak out the front door.

The beam from Alan's flashlight cuts the outside black in half. We hold hands when we tiptoe through the wet and squishy grass. Crickets chirp behind the black, and Mrs. Winthrop's house stares like a beast with yellow eyes. "Windows," Alan explains me about those square and scary eyes.

"They look mad." I shiver. "Maybe Mrs. Winthrop will be also mad."

But she isn't. Instead, she looks real surprised. Her eyes are boiled eggs bulging out at us now instead of fish, and her hands tie trembly knots in front her long, lacy bathrobe. "Why, Alan! Margaret!" Her voice still sounds all froggy. "Whatever are you children doing here, at this time of night?"

"We came to visit you," Alan says politely.

I add quick, "We promise to be good children. We'll be seen and not heard."

Mrs. Winthrop frowns at us. "Did your mother send you over here, dears?"

"Yes," I answer her, smiling. This is true. Mommy sent us yesterday, but we sneaked into the alley and played Star Wars instead. "We wanted to come our own selves anyways, though."

Mrs. Winthrop's frown flips up into a smile. This time it's not a pretend smile. "Why, I'm simply delighted," she says, and I can tell she really means it, too. "Come in, children!" So we do.

Mrs. Winthrop's living room looks filled with animals. Squirrels, birds, horses, frogs, and kitty-cats stand round on all the shelves and tables. They are not real ones, but the kind made from shiny stuff that breaks. We Look but Do Not Touch. Then Mrs. Winthrop says, "Choose something for yourselves, dears. These are old knickknacks, and I'm trying to get rid of them."

"Really?" We stare at her with open mouths, but she only smiles back at us and nods.

"Cool!" Alan shouts. He picks, from behind a ticking clock, a little twisty green glass snake. "Look, Pegasus." He waves it at me. "She does like snakes, after all."

But I say nothing, cause I just found a horse with wings. His wings look glowing orangey-pink like the sunset inside my seashell. The rest of him is cloudy milk but cept for eyes, which are black as the night outside. I pick him up and show him to Mrs. Winthrop. "That's Pegasus," she tells me, smiling. "I know that, dear. I've done my research now. I placed him just where I hoped you'd find him if you came."

"Can I really keep him? Oh, Mrs. Winthrop!" I hug her when she nods. "Why are you being so nice to us?"

Her face sags into sad little pockets, crisscrossed with about a million spiderwebs. She does look like a bag, one that turned all crinkly from being smashed. She almost answers me, but right then Alan bounces over. "Mrs. Winthrop, we got presents for you, too."

She likes his Saturn rock and my waterless daisies almost as much as we like her animals. Her sad spiderwebs jump back up into happy ones. Even the bug on her nose looks happy. It dances there whenever she laughs. "I've been lonely these many years," she says. "I never dreamed before tonight that children could be so—refreshing."

I ask, "Were you ever a child, Mrs. Winthrop?"

Alan laughs at my question, almost hard as Mrs. Winthrop does. But even he looks surprised when she shows us the pictures in her big brown crunchy book.

One is of a my-sized little girl. She wears a lacy dress that poofs out like a bell and a hairbow almost bigger than her head. Her hairs spill down her back in curly peelings same as mine. Her eyes look big and staring, but like moons instead of eggs or fishes. And smack on top her nose there sits a tiny brown bug.

"Is that you?" I point to the little girl in the picture, then look up at the big bug on Mrs. Winthrop's nose.

The big bug dances when she nods.

That picture is my favorite. Alan's favorite one is of a him-sized boy waving a speckledy lizard. "My brother Robert," Mrs. Winthrop explains. "He liked the crawling things, too. But I always preferred cats and horses."

"Me too." I feel sparkly inside. "And is this one your big sister?" I point to a picture of a Caitlin-sized girl, wearing two dark circles on her cheeks. Her hairs are piled up in a tower top her head, and her hand clutches the hand of a her-sized boy. He gots wings instead of hairs in front his face.

"No, that one also is of me," she answers with a rainy smile. "With my first sweetheart, Tom." Then I see the bug on the big girl's nose. Her sweetheart Tom has not a bug, only a sharky smile. He looks kind of like Caitlin's boyfriend Hairy Barry, but cept without fur on his face.

"He reminds me," Alan whispers to me when Mrs. Winthrop slips off to put away her book. "We better get home before they notice we're gone."

"Okay," I say. So we do. But not before Mrs. Winthrop gives us lemon cake with tea. And not before we

A NOT-REALLY GROWN-UP

tell her we love her—cause she's not a really grown-up, after all.

Nobody else is back yet when we sneak into our house. Brandi and her friends are all still there, drinking Cokes and jumping to Caitlin's music. We put ourselves to bed and I fall asleep with my dress on, holding Pegasus in my arms. (I mean not myself, but the shiny horsey one with wings.) I dream that me and Alan ride that horse to Mrs. Winthrop's. We pick up Mrs. Winthrop too and sail over a screaming fence. Then we snap pictures of Brandi's friends jumping down below.

The next morning—boy, is Mommy mad! But only cause Brandi and her friends ate up all our food . . . plus filled the whole house with empty Cokes.

5.

MAKING THINGS UP

My friend Haley lives next door. She lives not in the gray house with Mrs. Winthrop, but in the yellow house where is the other next door. Haley's mommy lives there too. She is Mommy-sized but cept for her tummy, which gots a tiny baby living inside.

Haley is sized like me. But she likes to play the grown-up part—the Teacher or the Mommy. I like to play the far-away part—the platypus with polka dots or the unicorn from Venus.

"Those things are just silly, Margaret-pargaret," Haley argues. She says that with hands on her hips, her eyes staring at me like bossy brown marbles. "They're not even real. And anyways, I'd rather play with Barbies."

We argue about our Barbie dolls, too. Haley pretends they're fashion models going out on dates. I pretend they're cave girls who are visiting Earth from ancient Neptune.

"Those things are even sillier," she tells me. "You just made them up. You're not s'posed to make things *up*, you're only s'posed to *make* things."

Haley likes to make things—snowflakes and bead-rings and twisty paper chains. Her fingers act cleverer than mine. "Fingers are to make things with, silly," she argues when I tell her we are both five fingers old. "We are five *years* old, not five fingers." We play together a lot, but we argue a lot too.

Haley gots a favorite song. It goes, "Anything you can do, I can do better."

She sings this loud when she climbs up high on top the jungle gym.

She brags it when she ties her own shoestrings.

She sings it soft when she cuts out paper dolls, showing me how she never chops off their heads.

And she whispers it when she colors inside the lines.

Coloring is what Haley likes to do best. She dumps all my color-books onto the rug beside my bed. "There," she says with a fat smile. "Now we can color. You pick out the crayons, Margaret-pargaret."

"Okay, Haley-paley." I pull out my crayon box from under my bed, a box like Alan's but cept not with bugs inside. (Mommy says one bug box is enough for any family.) My crayon box holds two kinds of crayons. I always pick for Haley the fat and blurry ones with their paper skins teared off. I take the new kind, skinny and sharp and smarter at staying inside the lines. But it doesn't help. Haley knows this good as me, and she takes whatever I give.

Coloring is the same old thing. Back and forth, up and down, round and round and round. Soon my hand feels tired, and then my crayon jumps. It zigs a twisty line, clean across the page. "Now look what you've done," Haley always scolds. She shakes a finger at me, just like Mommy or Caitlin.

I stare at the ziggy line and think. "That's Modern Art," I say at last. "Daddy showed me some in a book." Or, "That's a beam from a phaser gun on *Star Trek,* like what Alan watches. It just stunned the Papa Smurf."

"I don't believe you, Margaret-pargaret," Haley always argues. "You're just making that up."

One day this gives me an idea. "Let's just make things up," I say. "Let's draw our own pictures and make our own color book. That will be more fun."

Haley stares at me like I got a horn sprouting from my forehead. Her face looks like a paper without words or pictures there, and her eyes are brown marble questions.

This time *I* give *her* a fat smile. "You can pick out the crayons, Haley-paley. I'll go get some papers."

So she does and I do. My papers live in a secret book Daddy gave me last month for my birthday. I hide this book in my sock drawer, which is like the one where Alan once kept his stuffed bird Pluto. Now I dig under socks for it so Haley cannot see. I tear out some still-empty papers from the back.

Haley picks for herself the sharp and skinny crayons. But this time I don't care. Her face still looks empty, like the papers I drop in front of us. "What we gonna draw?" She asks that in her whining skeeto voice.

"Let's draw people on other planets," I tell her. "You draw ones on Pluto, and I'll draw ones on Mars."

"That's dumb, those planets don't got people," Haley argues. "People only goed to the moon."

"That's Earth people," I explain. "Mars and Pluto peoples are what I mean, peoples who live there and are different from the people here."

Haley wrinkles up her nose. "You mean like E.T.?"

"Yes, but 'cept I don't think he's from Mars or Pluto. And plus, somebody else already 'magined him. I mean other-planet peoples we 'magined our *own* selves."

"Well, I still think it's dumb." Haley sniffs and shakes her head. *"You* couldn't 'magine peoples like that. I think you're just making them up!"

I smile even fatter. "Well, that's exactly what I said—right, Haley-paley? 'Let's just make things up.' "

"Well, I bet you can't *draw* them."

"Bet *you* can't."

"I can too." Haley's eyes scrinch up into flashing pins. Tomato juice swims over her face, the way it does on

Caitlin when she's mad. "I can do *anything* better'n you!" She grabs her a skinny sharp crayon and points it down against her paper. Her mouth turns into a pink stick with white puckers round its edges. When she stares down at her paper, two more pink sticks write themselves between her pin-shaped eyes.

I watch her awhile and smile. Then I grab me a blurry blue crayon and begin to draw.

I draw both Mars and Pluto peoples. Mars people look like giant earthworms, only blue with ten red eyes. They dig houses under the ground, in holes between the purple Mars grasses.

Pluto people look like little marbles with green fur. They float inside pink bubbles, which jump out the silver Pluto grass whenever the planet burps.

I draw some Jupiter people, too. They are golden boxes with triangles for wings.

All three planet peoples are having a picnic on the moon. I draw them drinking lemonade from a giant see-through glass. Space lemonade looks black, with little white stars sparkling inside. It tastes like licorice, but I don't know how to draw a taste.

"All done," I call out at last. I throw down my blurry black crayon and hold up my drawing. "Want to see?"

"No!" Haley yells. She squeezes shut her eyes and walks backwards on her knees, her drawing pressed flat against her tummy. "I saw yours already, and I still think it's dumb. Nobody else'd ever 'magine peoples like that—never in a million, zillion years."

"What kind did you draw?"

Haley only shakes her head, her eyes still squeezed tight shut. Suddenly she slams her hands together with the drawing sticked between. The paper crunches up, gets rolled into a crinkly little ball. Haley throws the ball. It bounces smack against a bed-leg, then plops down on the rug right front of me.

"No!" Haley yells again when I pick up the ball. But I go ahead uncrumpling it anyways. The opened-out paper looks filled with little crinkles. But I see nothing beneath those crinkles—no pictures or words or even ziggy lines. Haley's paper looks plain-white empty—empty as her face looked when she asked me what to draw.

Then I hear a sniffle.

I look up and there lays Haley, rolled into a ball same as her drawing. The Haley-ball sniffles and snuffs, shivering like Jell-O. Tears squirt out her squeezed-shut eyes, spilling tween her fingers pressed flat against her face. "I don't care," she says between her sniffles. "So you can draw better'n me. So what?"

"It's okay," I tell her, patting her messed-up yellow hairs. "Want to cut out some paper dolls?"

Haley slowly unballs herself. She sits back up and blows her nose on the bottom stripe of her T-shirt. Her hands brush smooth her hairs till they look like an upside-down bowl, and at last she smiles like rainy sun. "Okay, Margaret-pargaret."

So I run get the paper dolls from my toybox underneath the window. I grab my scissors too, and I give Haley the unsticking ones. We spread everything out on my rug top of everything else—the crayons and the color books and the papers filled with pictures or just crinkles.

We smile when we cut, when Haley cuts her dolls out straight along the dotted lines. I cut mine all crookedy, but she doesn't sing her song. And she doesn't even scold me when I chop off some more heads.

6.

THE SECRET OF HAVE AND BRAVE

"Am I really going to school like Alan and Caitlin? Will I really learn science and square roots and social studies?"

"Slow down, baby." Daddy laughs. "Sure you will, but not all the first year. First you've got to learn how to read and write."

I smile and clap closed tight my mouth. So Daddy doesn't know my secret, after all. I can still make it a surprise.

The store is stuffed with clothes and notebooks and lunchboxes, toys and noise and boys, and two kinds of peoples—both real and statue ones. Signs everywhere say BACK TO SCHOOL. Me and Alan and Mommy swim through the holes between the peoples.

Alan wants to look at only turtles and computers. I want to look at everything cept itchy sweaters. Mommy holds on tight to both our hands. "I'm getting fed up with both of you," she whispers tween her teeth. "Now please behave!"

"Who is Have?" Alan asks. But Mommy doesn't answer him.

"Look!" I shout, pointing. "Over there's Haley with her mommy!"

"Don't point," Mommy whispers, but they come swimming toward us anyways.

"Hi, Haley-paley!"
"Hi, Margaret-pargaret!"
"Are you shopping for school-pool?"
"Are you plopping in the swimming pool?"

We laugh and dance each other around, banging into peoples.

"*Shhhh!*" Mommy-hands grab our arms and shake us apart.

"*Shhhh* is a grown-up word," Haley tells me, puffing out her chest. She always does that when she wants to look important. "It means whisper, like when somebody is pregnant."

"*Shhhh* is what the wind says when it swims through trees at night. My mommy is a tree."

"*My* mommy is pregnant. Soon I will be a big sister."

"I'm already a horse with wings."

"Are not."

"Am too."

"Are *not!*"

"Am *too!*"

Mommy-hands again yank us apart. "I told you to behave," my mommy scolds when she shakes me. "Can't you act right in a public place?"

Haley's mommy doesn't scold or shake. She only laughs and groans and says, "You little monster!" Then she scoops up Haley on top of her tummy filled with baby.

"Sometimes, only sometimes," I whisper sad to Alan, "I wish me and Haley could switch mommies."

"Yes, Pegasus." Alan nods and breathes out wind, his leaf-eyes looking rainy while they stare at those computers. "I think I understand what you mean."

The two mommies talk about Haley's daddy, who ran away last April with another lady when he found out her mommy was pregnant. I know what *pregnant* means, but still my mommy whispers. And she shakes her finger at me and Alan when we try to listen.

Then more peoples swim between us and swallow us apart. Haley and her mommy get goned away from us.

We swim along with those other peoples, turning even hurrier as we pick more stuff for school.

But even so, Mommy lets me wear my new pink running shoes that squeak. And she buys for Alan the little box with numbers he wants, the baby computer he calls a calculator. When we all stop to drink chocolate shakes at the long table with spinning stools, I know right then I wouldn't switch my mommy for anyone. Not even a mommy horse with wings.

Then back come Haley and her mommy, swimming with us out the doors that open by themselves. "I got a brand-new Strawberry Shortcake lunchbox," Haley says in her bragging voice.

"Me and Alan got E.T.'s."

"That's dumb, Margaret-pargaret. E.T.'s just for boys-poys."

"Is not."

"Is too!"

"Is *not!*"

"Enough, young lady." Mommy grabs my arms and shakes me hard once more. Then she spanks me on my bottom—twice and even harder. "That's what you get when you don't behave."

"Who is Have?" I ask this time, after I finish crying.

Mommy doesn't answer me either.

"Be brave," Mommy says.

The fat and furry doctor wipes my arm with warm wet cotton. The needle's poking up from his fat and furry hand. "Just relax, honey," he says to me, smiling. "It'll all be over in a second."

"And then we'll go get ice cream." Mommy sounds a little bit too cheerful. "So just relax and be brave like Alan was."

Alan stands there staring at some sharp and pointy things, silver sticks that sparkle on a table side of me. Now he turns and smiles sparkly at me when I moan. "It's really interesting, Pegasus," he says. "It's a Salk vaccination. The doctor will stick bacteria in your arm. They're a species sort of like these very tiny bugs—"

"Alan, please." Mommy shivers. I shiver too, but not cause I don't like Alan talking about bugs. It's cause that is when the needle gets sticked into my arm, stinging like a long and silver bee.

"Careful, Pegasus," Mommy says afterwards in the ice cream place. "You're dripping that cone all over your brand-new sweater."

"That's okay, 'cause the sweater's only an itchy one. Mommy?" I ask her when she scrubs me with her napkin. "Why do you always want me to Be Have or to Be Brave? Why can't I just be *me?*"

"But you *are* you, my dear." Mommy shakes her head at me and smiles. "You are already my Margaret Elizabeth, alias Pegasus the Incorrigible."

"What means 'In Core Jable'?"

Mommy doesn't answer me. I think this is cause she didn't understand my question. My mouth's too filled with ice cream—parts I bited off to stop them raining down my hands.

Mommy takes me to Register at Alan's school. Register is a little room of tall gray shiny boxes. A desk sits front of these with a lady sticked behind. Kids and other grown-ups sit on a long brown woody board against one wall. Books fill up another wall instead of clocks or pictures, and crunchy papers pile up on the desk.

Mommy writes on some of those papers for about a million years. I sing about a million times, "Did You Ever See a Board Walk?" (Even though the board underneath ns doesn't.) I sing that till the desk lady frowns and Mommy whispers, *"Shhhh!"*

"But it's so boarding here," I complain.

"You mean boring, babe?"

"No, *board*ing. That means tired of sitting here on this long hard board."

Mommy laughs. She's in one of her happy moods, not her scolding ones. "We'll see what we can do about that," she tells me, standing up. She tiptoes to the desk and whispers to the lady. The desk lady gives her a little board with more papers sticked on top—but empty ones not with words or fill-in lines. Mommy brings this to me and she hands me a pencil, too. "Draw me a far-out Martian, babe."

I shake my head. "Crayons are for drawing. Pencils are for writing, just like you," I explain. "I will write you a story instead."

Then I groan inside.

That was sposed to be a secret, a surprise!

I quick clap my hands over my mouth. But I can tell Mommy didn't even notice what I said. "That's fine, baby," she answers in her far-away voice—and she smiles like she does when she knows I'm just pretending.

I write a story anyways. I write it cause it fills my head and has to squeeze on out. I write it cause it's *board*ing to draw things not with color crayons. Plus I want to be like Mommy, who is writing on papers too.

Once there were two sisters named Have and Brave.

Have got spanked by Mommy in a store.

Brave got sticked with needles by a doctor. They were filled with tiny bugs.

One day Have said, "I don't want to be me. Can't I be you instead?"

"Okay," said Brave. "And I'll be you."

So they did.
When Mommy and the doctor came they couldn't tell which was which.
So they said, "Let's mix them up and make only one girl."
And they did.
And the only one girl was ME.
Pegasus the In Core Jable!

I want to keep my story—which gots realife words made from realife letters in—a secret. So here is how I do this. After finishing the real story, I write a pretend one—a story filled with only dots and lines and squiggles. And this is the one I'll give to Mommy when she's done.

Mommy gets done same time as me. She stands up and steps over to hand her papers to the lady. I grab my papers from the big sit-on board, where I dropped them right next to an Alan-sized boy. I fold them up and stuff them into the pocket of my jacket, then hand back my small board to the lady.

The desk lady smiles and thanks me. Then she frowns over at the Alan-sized boy, who's slumped down on the board with his legs sprawling out. (He looks like he thinks it's boarding too.) "Young man!" she scolds him. "You get back to your assignment!"

The Alan-sized boy scoops up some papers from his lap, begins to read them. Then he grins a sharky smile. Cold shivers swim down my arms, cause that boy-poy smiles same as Hairy Barry.

"Hey!" he yells suddenly, real loud. "This ain't my assignment, lady. Who the freak is 'Pegasus the In Core Jable?'"

More cold shivers swim through me. I pull my papers back out my pocket and unfold them. Then I feel freezed, cause I can tell right away they're *not* my story.

The top one says, MITCHELL BRANNON, SUMMER SESSION DETENTION. And beneath that, I WILL NOT TALK BACK IN CLASS, printed over and over down the page.

I dart over to the boy and switch papers with him. Then I skip back to Mommy, grab hold tight her hand. She stares down at me about a million years, and the look inside her eyes makes me think she guessed my secret.

"Pegasus," she says on our way home. "Did you *really* write me a story back there?"

"Yes." I hand her the pretend one that is filled with only dots and lines and squiggles. Mommy reads it head-shaking, but she asks me no more questions. She only smiles at me and says how nice.

At home I sneak the real story into my secret birthday book. Then I pull my crayons out and draw Mommy a far-out Martian.

7.

KIDNEY GARDEN

My first day of school, Alan walks me all the way.

We run, skip, and jump into piles of crunchy brown leaves. The on-tree leaves look red and gold and orange, same as my hairs. The wind smells like it's mixed with smoke that floats all stinging up our noses. We laugh and race to catch the leaves that swim on top the wind, spank them with our new notebooks and E.T. lunchboxes. But they only dart away and laugh at us. "Leaves think people are silly," I tell Alan.

Caitlin thinks little kids are silly. I know cause she and Brandi walk in front of us real fast, till they turn into tiny specks. Their talking is the kind that pretends we are not there, so we pretend they are invisible bacterias.

"Hi, Haley-paley!" I wave to my friend as she catches up to us. "Want to walk with us?" But Haley does not answer my question or wave back. Instead, she wraps both arms round her mommy's tummy filled with baby. The mommy waves in her place. Then she unhooks Haley and grabs tight to one of her hands.

"I'll see you later by yourself, Margaret-pargaret," Haley whispers loud to me when they squeeze past us. "But I'm not walking to school with any dumb ol' boy-poy, poy-boy!" She skips on ahead, swinging her Strawberry Shortcake lunchbox and her mommy's arm.

Alan looks at me with questions in his eyes. "Is Haley mad at me?" he asks. "What difference does it make if I'm a boy?"

"I don't know. Maybe she feels jealous 'cause you're my brother. *Her* brother's still inside her mommy's tummy."

"Or sister," Alan reminds me. "But that does sound logical, Pegasus." He smiles at me then, and he takes my hand when we cross the big street in front the school.

The school looks like a square red beast with lots of window-eyes. The other kids are giant bugs the beast swallows whole and barfs. They come in all shapes and sizes. They push and run and yell. Suddenly some Alan-sized boys yell at us. "Alan's got a girlfriend! Alan's got a girlfriend!" They yell that about a million times.

"I am not his girlfriend, but his sister," I explain. But those silly boys-poys won't listen.

Tomato juice swims over Alan's face. "Just ignore them," he whispers to me between his teeth. He squeezes my hand tighter. Then he drags me over to a giant caterpillar, wriggling around in front of two big doors. The caterpillar's made up of a million my-sized children. "Here's your kidney-garden class," Alan whispers, letting go my hand. "See you later, Pegasus." He races off before I can say goodbye.

"Boy, is Alan dumb." The caterpillar part in front of me turns round, and I see it has a Haley head. "You got the dumbest brother I know."

"Alan is not dumb," I argue to that Haley. "Mommy and Daddy say he is a genius."

"Do not."

"Do too!"

"Do *not!*"

Our voices get drowned inside the other kids' voices. The whole caterpillar is arguing or laughing or jumping or splitting into parts. At last its head—the *real* head at its very front—turns round. It looks like a furry grown-up lion. The lion roars, "Cool it, you characters!" And the caterpillar goes all still and quiet.

Just then the bell rings like a giant's burp. The two doors swing wide open, and in we wriggle—that whole long caterpillar, with me and Haley sticked smack in its middle and the furry grown-up lion at its front. "Let's scoot!" he calls, and we scoot down the long clangy hall to our room.

The room called kidney garden is not a garden at all. It doesn't have any kidneys, either. I see only plants in pots and a glass box full of fishes, sticked on top a board against the window. Pictures live on the walls, and lights live on the ceiling. The floor carries baby tables and chairs with toys dropped all around, just like in my Sunday School class. The piano looks the same as the ones in Sunday School and at my house.

That roaring grown-up lion who headed up the caterpillar is our teacher. He looks like Daddy, but cept with a midnight-black mane curling round his head stead of an orange one. Also he is skinnier, and he jumps around lots more. "You can call me Skip," he tells us, jumping with his voice. "And that is just what we're going to do right now."

Skip doesn't skip. He only plays the piano, while everybody else skips in a circle round the room. But his piano song skips from underneath his fingers as they skip up and down the teeth. "I can skip better than her," Haley tells him afterwards, pointing straight at me. Then she says, being fair, "But she can draw better."

Drawing is what we do next.

"Draw a picture of anything you like," Skip tells us. Haley groans just then, but I feel sparkly inside. "Afterwards we'll each get a turn to tell about our pictures—and something about ourselves."

The crayons are all new ones, sharp and skinny. Even so, Haley does not look happy. "What am I gonna draw?" she asks me, whining same as always. I stop and think a minute, then whisper an idea. "That's dumb!" She groans again, same as always. But I don't argue with her, cause Haley always draws whatever I say.

I think some more ideas for my own picture. At last I pick an idea and a crayon. The crayon is a black one, so sharp and skinny it looks almost like a pencil. And that is what gives me my idea.

I will share my special secret, make it a surprise.

I will *write* my picture, stead of drawing it!

The other kids all draw. They make houses and flowers and cars and even starships, but no blue Martians with ten red eyes. One boy with hairs like sticking-up grass makes only crinkles that got spaces in between. He cries the same way Haley did when she drew only crinkles at my house.

Haley's turn comes first, to share her picture with the class.

"This is a kidney garden." She says it real soft, staring down at the floor and hiding the paper with her hands. "It is a garden that grows kidneys."

"Say it one more time, Haley, a little louder." Skip smiles at her, leaning forward. "And show everyone your picture."

She holds it up, a green box filled with lots of long red dots. When she says again what is it, some of the kids laugh.

Haley's face folds up into a wrinkly tomato. "Of course I know that's not what it means really," she says, sniffing. "A kidney garden really just means this class—the baby class. This dumb picture was *her* idea." Haley-paley again points straight at me.

I feel all burny inside my cheeks. I want to poof away like smoke from those burning leaves outside. All the kids are turned around, staring at me. Only Skip stares at Haley instead. "Next time, Haley," he says, "let's hear *your* idea." Then his stare does switch to me. "And as for you, Free Thinker—from now on save those ideas for yourself." His stare melts into a smile. "Got another one to share?"

I gulp and then nod. My burny feeling is melting too, turning into sparkly. I say, "If you mean it's my turn now to share, I got to read my picture 'stead of talking it."

Skip's eyes look like Mommy's when she thinks I'm just pretending. But he smiles same as Daddy, so I begin.

> *Pegasus*
> *A horse with wings*
> *That is who I am.*
> *My wings are pink with lions and birds.*
> *I learn about rats in mazes*
> *But write stories about clouds.*
> *My stories were a secret*
> *And the horse is still pretend.*
> *My realiſe name is*
> *Margaret Elizabeth Kendall.*

When I finish, Skip just stares at me again. Milk swims over his face and eats up all his smile. He says, "Let me see that paper." I take it up to him, feeling crawly inside now. The other kids' eyes are Daddy's nails, hammered into my back. Skip's eyes are two more nails, hammered into my paper. His head shakes several times. At last he asks, "Did you write this all by yourself?"

"Yes." I dart back to my chair.

Haley next to me looks freezed. "Boy, are you in trouble," she whispers. "You were s'posed to write a *picture,* not a story."

I don't answer her. Just then Skip's furry hand lands on my shoulder. But he smiles like Daddy again, and his voice when it comes sounds like soft wind. "Margaret, who taught you how to read and write?"

I tell the truth. "Me. I taught myself."

"That's a lie!" That is Haley. "I hate you, Margaret Kendall! Now everybody's gonna like *you* better'n me. It's not *fair*—"

"Haley. Cool it." Skip uses his lion voice on her, then turns to me and talks soft wind again. "Pegasus, I really need to know." Then he asks, "May I call you Pegasus?"

The whole class explodes.

"Pegasus!" yells the grass-haired boy. "That's a *nerdy* name!"

"Yeah!" yells his friend. "It's *gross!*"

"It's *yukka!*"

"It's *dumb!*"

Everybody laughs and yells, and I feel like disappearing into air. "Cool it, you characters!" Skip roars again, just like a lion.

But this time nobody listens to him.

"She's a *liar!*" The grass-haired boy yells that, pointing straight at me.

Suddenly Haley spins around and clonks him on the nose. The boy falls out his chair, and she jumps on top his tummy. Her fingers roll up into stones and hammer down his face. "Take *that,* you dumb ol' boy-poy!"

Skip scrunches down and scoops her off the boy. "Take it easy, Haley," he says, standing her on her feets. "Violence is uncool."

"I don't care." Haley frowns up at him, hands on her hips. "I don't like ol' boys-poys." She sniffs and brushes down her hair-bowl. "Pegasus *is* a dumb name, I think so too. And Margaret-pargaret, she's always making things up. But she is *still* my best friend."

I jump up and hug her. "You're my best friend too, Haley-paley!"

The grass-haired boy just lays there and cries. The other kids are laughing at *him* now. Even his best friend is laughing at him.

Skip stares at us a long-long time. He shakes his shaggy head, breathing like a giant wind. His face looks like a giant question about all of us.

But mostly, I think, about me.

8.

WORRIED

"I worry about her going into the third grade."

Mommy really does sound worried. I can hear her voice floating from the living room into the kitchen, where I'm sitting at the speckledy table doing pretend homework. I stop writing so's I can listen.

"Those bigger kids can be rough. And she is still so little."

"Relax, baby." That is Daddy's voice, hugging Mommy like his furry arms. "Our Pegasus can charm the socks off a snake."

"James." Mommy's voice again, a slicing silver knife. "You planned this all along, didn't you? You taught her yourself, from those everlasting books of yours."

"Oh, Lisa!" Daddy's voice, a blurry boom. "I read to her, yes. I planted in her a love for books, a fascination with language, a desire to soar on the wings of her imagination—"

"Really, James!"

"But the rest of it," Daddy goes on, "she did all on her own. I swear it. Pegasus," he calls, poking his lion head round the kitchen door. "Come tell Mommy how you taught yourself to read."

"Okay, Daddy." I slide down from my chair and hop into the living room. I got to hop on both my feets, not like Haley who can hop on only one. But Haley, I remember, can't write stories.

They plop me down in the the fat green chair, then both smile at me. Mommy smiles with more worried and Daddy with more proud. I begin the telling, smiling back at them.

"When I was only three fingers old, I thought words were bugs like in Alan's box. Magic bugs that didn't crawl, instead they told people stories, but by thinking and not talking. The grown-ups just say out loud, I thought, whatever the bugs think to them. Or else they just remember.

"But one day I saw Caitlin reading with her finger. She was pointing at each bug and whispering a word. 'Are you saying the bugs' names?' I asked her. But she said, 'Those aren't bugs, dummy. Those are words.'

" 'You mean the words people *talk?'* I asked her. So she groaned like she always does and said, 'Of course, you little pest. Go ask Daddy to explain it to you.' So I did and he did—"

"James!" Mommy interrupts. She jumps her eyebrows at Daddy.

But he only smiles bigger and shakes his head. "Go on, Pegasus."

"Daddy just explained me Caitlin's right," I go on. "The bugs themselves are words like people say. So that night when he read to me, I pointed out each word with my finger. I matched the seeing words with talking ones. And I kept on doing this for every night and day and night again, for a long, long time until I turned five fingers old like now. And now I know them all."

Daddy and Mommy both laugh, sounding like lions and birds at the same time. Then they pull me into a hug. "Nobody knows them all," Daddy says. "You've still got a lot to learn, Pegasus."

"I know, Daddy. But Skip said I'd learn it better in the third grade."

"Oh, baby." Mommy begins to cry. "That's what you really want, isn't it?"

"Yes. But don't worry, Mommy." I wipe her eyes with my fingers. "I'll charm the socks off a snake if you want me to." I think about this. "Daddy, how can snakes wear socks when they don't got any feets?"

"What?" Daddy's face jumps under his orange mane.

"And do 'maginations wear wings," I ask too, "the same as birds and horses?"

Mommy's crying turns back into laughing. Grown-ups but cept Caitlin always laugh when I ask questions. This time it only makes me happy. I smile when she laughs, when Daddy explains me about *metaphors*. "So those are words that pretend you're something else?" I ask him, to make sure. "Like Mommy is a tree full of birds and curly leaves, and you're a big orange laughing lion?"

"You've got it... my little horse with wings." Daddy grins and gently tugs my hair-carrots, his eyes all relaxed with glowy-proud. Mommy smiles too, but she doesn't look relaxed. Above her smile, her eyes still cry with worried.

"Let's not hold hands anymore around the school. Okay, Pegasus?"

Alan looks worried too. He strides next to me like a grown-up—not skipping, not running, not jumping in the piles of crunchy brown leaves. I don't jump in those leaves either this morning. The leaves that are Alan's eyes look rainier than usually.

"The boys in my class are mean sometimes," he whispers to me now. "When I take you into the room, they'll prob'ly say you are my girlfriend."

"They're just silly," I whisper back, remembering those boys. "They're not good listeners. Besides, girlfriends are for big boys sized like Peter. I wish Caitlin liked *him* 'stead of Hairy Barry."

"Me too." Alan smiles. "Peter's cool! I think he just scares Caitlin 'cause he's different."

"Daddy says everybody's different."

"He's right, Pegasus. But some people are more different than others." Alan shakes his head, breathing like a wind. "I wish sometimes I wasn't. It's hard, being different—'specially in third grade. You'll find out, Pegasus. Third grade can be pretty rough."

"Don't worry, Alan." I hug his closest arm. "We'll just pretend those boys are snakes with feets and charm their socks. Then I'll turn me into a horse with wings and fly us to the clouds. Anyways, I'll protect you, Alan—"

"No!" Alan yanks his arm away and darts ahead of me like he's being chased. Tomato juice swims up the back of his neck. "You can't protect me, you're too little," he explains, breathing hard when I catch up. "And I'm too little to protect you also, actually. If only Peter were here—"

"Yes! Peter!" I clap my hands, spin in a circle. "He'll protect us, he is big enough."

"That's not logical, Pegasus." Alan grabs my arms to slow me down. "Peter is starting high school today, like Caitlin. He won't be around for us this year."

"That's okay." I jump into a pile of crunchy leaves. "We'll *pretend* he's with us, and that will feel the same."

"It's an interesting theory, Pegasus." But Alan doesn't jump along with me into those leaves. The ones that are his eyes still swim with worried.

"You certainly can read, Margaret."

Mrs. Stone gives me a trembly smile. She takes from me her skinny book with its story about a pancake. I feel worried about a fox eating up that poor pancake, cause it could run and talk the same as me.

Mrs. Stone looks worried about *me.*

"If only you weren't such a *little* girl," she keeps saying. "Oh dear, oh dear . . ." She washes her hands without soap, the same way Peter does. They are wrinkly-speckledy hands that look like Mrs. Winthrop's.

Mrs. Stone is not a stone, she's Alan's third grade teacher. The really stone was Mr. Johns, who gave me those tests in the little room called the Resource Room. Tests are games, but scary ones that tell how smart you are. Alan and Daddy explained me this, not that old stone-faced Mr. Johns. Tests are also why I'm here, not in the kidney garden with Skip who is a lion.

Mrs. Stone is *not* a lion, any more than she's a stone. She looks more like a hippo, and she plogs instead of jumping. *(Plog* means *plod* and *drag* mixed up together. I made this word myself.) Her nose has not a bug, but she reminds me anyways of Mrs. Winthrop. I think she is not used to my-sized children who can read.

"Dear, do you know your multiplication tables?"

"No." I smile big at her. "I just know our kitchen and coffee tables. But I can count to ten."

"Oh dear, oh dear!" Mrs. Stone looks like she wants to cry. I reach out and pat her back, which feels like Jell-O with a bone inside.

"Don't worry, Mrs. Jell-O," I comfort her without thinking. "Alan can teach me those tables. They are actually not tables but numbers, and he knows 'bout more numbers than are stars in the universe."

Alan's teacher gives me a wobbly smile. "You certainly are Alan's sister," she says, shaking her head. "You should be proud of your big brother, Margaret. He is a brilliant boy—the best in mathematics I've ever had. Now, if only I could teach him to read—"

"I'll teach him," I say real quick. "I'll teach him words, and he can teach me numbers. We'll trade what we know, okay? That way we will both know everything."

Mrs. Stone stares down at me, her eyes swimming like Jell-O stirred with spoons. Suddenly she pulls me into a big hug. Her arms are jiggly Jell-O too, but her blue dress feels all scratchy. It smells same as my itchy new sweater.

    Mrs. Stone doen't kiss me and make spit on my face like Mrs. Winthrop. And she doesn't get mad cause I called her Mrs. Jell-O. She only smiles at me Jell-O-ly. But her eyes above her smile still swim with worried.

9.

OBSERVING

"Children can be quite interesting," I say to Mrs. Stone.

We sit together on the shiny blue bench against the playground fence. The other kids are snakes across that playground, blurry snakes with socks and feets and yelling mouths. All but cept my brother, who's a quiet cat instead. He crouches behind the swing set with his magnifying glass, observing how the ants climb up the grasses.

"I like to observe children." I also like to use *observe,* the new word Alan taught me. "Observing is quite interesting, too. Alan observes animals and bugs and rocks and leaves and stars and planets. But I prefer observing human children."

"That's nice, dear." Mrs. Stone's eyes look worried at me above her trembly smile. "But wouldn't you like to *play* with the children?"

"No, thank you." I smile back real big to hide my crawly feeling inside. "I'd rather just sit here with you and observe them. That way I can see everything they're doing all at once. Not just one song or game or climb, or just one hitting 'tween those boys-poys, but everything—the all of it—all at the same time."

This is true, but it's not the whole-thing true. I do not explain to her the other truc, the part that makes those worms swim through my tummy in pickle juice. And I do not explain what makes the water splash behind my knees. The water inside her eyes already looks too worried now. Those worried eyes always swim at Alan too—Alan when he gets called names or punched by Mitchell Brannon.

"Nerd Bird! Bug Brain! Little Professor Weirdo!"

That's what they call my brother, that mean old Mitchell Brannon and his yucky friends with mud. They throw the mud at Alan in globs that stripe his shirt, but Alan never throws some back. He only slinks away, his cheeks the color of tomato juice.

One day I throwed at Mitchell a book-sized glob of mud, all filled with bugs. That's after I first heard him say "Bug Brain" to my brother. But Alan didn't like me doing this. "Don't you see that makes him even worse?" He hissed that like a mad cat in the corner. "Please don't try to protect me, Pegasus. It's best if we just ignore him."

"Okay, Alan," I promised. And I did—for about five minutes. But sometimes Ignore feels harder than stones or bones or multiplication tables.

"Pegasus the Puke! Weirdo's Weirder Sister! Kidney Garden Baby!" Mitchell yelled those names at me. Then he pulled my braids apart and snarled, "Carrot Hair!"

"I never puke, and we are never weird," I explained to him logically. "I am not a baby, but a big girl in third grade. Besides, it's not polite to pull out hairs. Plus, your hairs are orange like mine, so I think they also got scraped from carrots."

This is all true. But that old Mitchell Brannon wouldn't listen to me. He only punched me—smack in my tummy.

And that is partly why I like better not to play, but rather to observe from the bench with Mrs. Stone.

If only Haley-paley were here, I think now from that bench. *She* would not Ignore those mean old boys-poys! (At least not for me. She still thinks Alan's dumb like other boys.) She'd clonk them on their noses like she did in the kidney-garden class, even if they are sized same as Alan stead of us. Then she'd climb up high on top the jungle gym and sing, "Anything you can do, I can do . . ."

Bzzzzzzzz.

That is not Haley, but the giant-burping bell. The bell means time to line up in the big long caterpillar, then go marching back inside our room of chalk and worlds and words. And back inside that room means Composition's coming next.

I feel sparkly now inside instead of crawly.

Third Grade Can Be Rough
by
Margaret Elizabeth Kendall
Room 102
Sept. 14, 1983

Third grade can be rough like my brother Alan said. The children run and climb and yell and punch and pinch. They are interesting, but violent like a war. Daddy explained us about war and it is bad. Skip who is a lion said, "Violence is uncool." Recess is my next to worst subject.

My really worst is math. It gots tables that you make from numbers, not from wood. I don't have to do those tables yet. Mrs. Stone lets me work on 1+1 and 2+2. But even those feel harder than a table made from stone.

I like reading best, about talking trains and horses and birds and pancakes. Plus, writing my own stories now that my secret's out. But I sure wish Mitchell Brannon never learned about my

"Your what, Carrot Hair?"

Mitchell asks me that in his awful snarling voice. His freckles glow like measles on his poofed-up bullfrog face, and his right hand grabs my pencil so's I cannot write some more. Then he yanks hard at my braids.

Ouch!

I say that "ouch" inside me—not out loud.

Mommy twists my long orange string-hairs into braids. I pretend my braids are curly carrots, soft ones that flop against my back like spaghettis. But usually those carrots break loose from their rubber bands and bows. Then they turn into wild lion-hairs, like the lion-hairs on Daddy. When their hairs are pulled, even lions can feel stings like getting burned.

Grrr! roars the lion inside me now—but not out loud. Outside me, I tell Mitchell what Skip said back in kidney garden. "Violence is uncool." But Mitchell only snarls—till he's interrupted by the teacher.

"Children, children!"

Mrs. Stone stands trembling in front her desk, tying her fat hands into knots. I wish she'd stop that Mitchell from stopping my Composition. She's too trembly-old to stop things usually. But this time she really does—with the someone who stands right next to her.

"Children," she says again in her trembly voice, hugging this someone to her Jell-O side. "I would like you to meet Sonia Gray. She is a new student to our class. Say 'hello' to Sonia, children. Say, 'Welcome to our class.' "

"Hello, Sonia. Welcome to our class!"

But only two kids say it.

Me and Alan.

The other kids just stare at Sonia with sagging-open mouths. They look like Alan's fishes, when my kitty Motorthroat taps the side of their glass bowl with her paw.

Sonia stares right back at us same way. Her mouth also sags open like those fishes. Her eyes look like those fishes too, swimming in close toward her nose. Like me, she is a different size from Alan and the other third graders. But cept she's bigger than them instead of smaller. She looks almost Caitlin-sized! But she doesn't act all bossy like my sister. Instead, she lets Mrs. Stone lead her to a seat. The teacher holds her hand, just like she is sized the same as me.

Everybody whispers now, but cept me and Alan. Some of the other kids laugh. They're quiet laughs, but they sound crawly like a bunch of hissing snakes. I shiver when those snake-laughs slither tween the rows of desks.

secret. I finish the last sentence of my Composition. But then I think and write some more.

Mitchell tried to stop this Composition, but then he got stopped instead. He got stopped by Mrs. Stone and Sonia coming here. If Mitchell stops Sonia from writing her Composition, I may have to act uncool and use violence on him.

That's because I like Sonia. I observed that she is interesting too.

10.

SONIA

"Eeeew! It's the *ree*-tard!"

That's what they call Sonia. Not just Mitchell Brannon does, but almost all the other kids—the whole third grade but cept for me and Alan.

"*Retard*'s just a piano lesson word," I comfort my new friend. "It means slow down, like catching your running breath."

"Actually, the musical term is *ritardando*," Alan says. "But *retard* does mean slow as well. Daddy explained it to me last night. However, in Sonia's case—Look out, Pegasus!"

I duck when the ball zings up, a fast white blur. It bounces off Alan's head. The ball's thrower laughs, because he's mean old Mitchell. "Two more retards!" he yells, meaning us this time.

At school me and Alan are almost the worst at everything. We're almost the worst at catching balls. And throwing balls. And climbing ropes (though Alan's good on trees). We're also almost the worst at cutting, pasting, and stringing paper chains.

Alan almost can't read yet. I almost can't add two plus two. And I still can't tie my shoestrings into bows. Before last week we really were the worst—at everything but cept for Alan, math and science, and for me, reading and writing and drawing pretend worlds.

Until Sonia came.

Sonia is now the worst at everything.

She can't catch or throw a ball or climb anything, read or write or draw or paste or do math problems either. She only sits and stares out from those eyes that almost fall into her nose. Then her head and back drop forward onto her desk. She looks sleeping but cept for one hand, gripping tight her pencil like a sword. She stabs her paper with that sword, making shaggy holes. The holes fill up with spit, spinning down in strings from her sagging-open mouth. This looks interesting, so I observe but do not laugh.

Me and Alan never laugh at Sonia. We know she is trying, same as us.

"Try," says Mrs. Stone, walking Sonia's hand. And Sonia tries with all of her, not just with her sword-gripped pencil. Her eyes try, scrinching up into little pins. Her tongue tries, poofing out and getting locked between her teeth. Sometimes an S comes out her pencil, backwards or too big. "Good girl!" Mrs. Stone says then, patting Sonia's head. And Sonia smiles like early sun exploding from a cave.

Mrs. Stone still smiles Jell-O-ly. One day after school she calls me and Alan to her desk. "Alan, Margaret." She whispers to us inside her stooped-down hug. "I've been watching you both with Sonia. You are kind and patient with her. You never torment her as the other children do. You seem to accept her, even though she's different."

"That's just 'cause we know how she feels," Alan explains. "See, me and Pegasus are different, too."

"God made everybody different," I add. "That's what Daddy says."

"Your daddy is quite correct," Mrs. Stone says in her trembling voice. "But some people are more different than others. I'm afraid Sonia is—one of God's special children."

"So that means she's the same as everyone else. Right, Mrs. Stone? 'Cause Daddy says we're *all* God's special children."

"Yes, well. That's, er, true enough, Margaret." Mrs. Stone's face turns pink like the inside of my seashell. "However, you and Alan are both extremely bright. In your separate ways, you two are the brightest students in my class. For this reason, I thought perhaps you might like to act as Sonia's tutors."

"But we are pounders, not tooters," I argue when Alan answers nothing. (He just turns pink like Mrs. Stone and stares down at his feets.) "Mr. Emmett, our piano teacher, always says I pound too hard and make mistakes. Besides, tooters toot on flutes and not pianos." I know this from my book of silly poems and tongue twisters. But when Mrs. Stone's trembling turns to laughing, I realize I just said something silly. A mistake.

"A mistake," Alan scolds me on our way home from school. But *he* does not mean about tooters. He means about my saying yes to Mrs. Stone.

"A *tutor*," she explained before we left, "is like a teacher, but with only one student. Sonia would be the student for you both. You'd work with her a bit every day after school. I thought perhaps that you, Alan, might help her learn her numbers. And you, Margaret, might help her learn to read."

"Okay." I felt sparkly inside.

But Alan only frowned and squeezed my hand. "I'm sorry, Mrs. Stone." He said that to his feets, his pink face turning the color of tomato juice. "But I—I'm too busy right now, helping Peter build Dileth's new maze. And— and Pegasus . . . We got to go now, anyways. It's almost time for her piano lesson."

Sometimes, only sometimes, I think as we plog on home, Alan is *not* my almost-favorite person in the world.

"It's a mistake, Pegasus," he argues now. "We can't afford to hang out with Sonia. Mitchell and those guys would pick on us worse than ever if we did. They *already* think we're weird. Can't you see that, Pegasus?"

"I see Sonia," I tell him instead. And I do just now. She's following after us with her head all hanging down, plogging same as us but cept not mad. Her face wears its glowy-sunrise smile, even when she trips over a waggling branch. "Hi, Sonia!" I call, smiling back and waving and slowing down for her. "Want to walk home with us?"

"Yes," she says in her blurry voice, plogging faster to catch up to us.

But Alan moves even faster. He fasts into a disappearing blur—right when Mitchell Brannon yells, "Retard!" from a tree.

"Fortissimo!" I yell up at him, forgetting to Ignore.

But then I freeze inside. Mitchell springs down from the tree, gripping the waggling branch. And after him jumps Jordan, then Trent and Tyler and Sean. All those boys clutch waggling branches, swing them like swords. All of them step forwards, their faces pulled into snarls.

"We're the Anti-Retard Brigade," Mitchell says as they move in closer. "We'll get you, Carrot Hair, *and* your retard friend. Better make like your Bug Brain brother an' start running!"

So I do—only *toward* them instead of away.

Grrr! roars the lion inside me.

And then the lion roars out loud!

The lion turns into me—or maybe me into the lion. My teeth stick out with points. My fingers all sprout claws, like the ones that sprout from Motorthroat's paws when she pounces at a bird. Mitchell is the bird now, then next come Trent and Tyler. Jordan and Sean are rats instead. Those mean gray skinny rats that live in garbage cans, not the snowy marshmallow kind like Dileth.

I pounce at all those birds and rats. "Take *that!*" I yell at them, like Haley would. But cept I yell in roaring lion language—and I don't have to clonk them on their noses.

Those bird-rat boys look so surprised they drop their waggling branches. Their faces swim with milk. Their eyes and mouths are circles, filled with squeaks instead of snarls. They start walking backwards, then turn and run away without me hitting. I think they didn't notice the lion was just pretend.

But Sonia knows. *"Issmo,* Peggy!" she shouts now, when we are by ourselves. *"Grrr,* Peggy! *Grrr!"* She laughs and claps, then locks me in a hug.

I smile at her smile and don't tell her to call me Pegasus. I know my whole pretend name is too hard for her to say. *"Grrr,* Sonia," I answer, hugging her back. *"Allegro! Andante!"* I teach her more piano words as we plog home together inch by inch.

But we plog home so snail-slow I'm late for my piano lesson.

And that is a *really* big mistake.

11.

THE LION INSIDE ME

"*One*-two-three. *One*-two-three. *One*-two-three."

That is Mr. Emmett talking, Mr. Emmett who gives me piano lessons. Mommy said third grade is big enough for taking those—even though I had not first a year of kidney garden, cause it only lasted me a week.

Mr. Emmett also is my teacher. But he's a different kind than Skip or Mrs. Stone. He teaches Caitlin as well as me and Alan, and his desk is our piano with its row of sparkling teeth. The piano's my desk, too. I sit there just two afternoons, when I come home from school.

Mr. Emmett looks like Peter Jenkins, skinny and with glasses on like two square-box windows. Only he's miles taller than Peter, and his skin looks smooth like milk instead of lumpy oatmeal. Behind his glasses, though, his eyes always swim at me with worried. "Oh dear, child," he says, trembling as he washes his soapless hands. "So many mistakes! You must go back to the beginning."

"Okay." But still I'd rather watch his fingers than the music. They look interesting, all trembly-long like Alan's earthworms. I observe them washing each other and make some more mistakes.

"Oh no, child!"

"I'm sorry, Mr. Emmett." I pet his back to comfort him, the way I pet my kitty. Sometimes he seems our-sized, cause when we make mistakes he turns all worried-sad like Peter. I like him a lot, but not his piano lessons. They are Something Else Again. Caitlin said to Mommy they are One Big Mistake.

I don't listen to old Caitlin, though. She also calls my being friends with Sonia a mistake. "Mother, must you let her hang around with that defective child?" She asked that only yesterday. "It's so embarrassing! I mean, Sonia's as old as me and my friends. She's hardly a suitable-aged friend for my five-year-old sister."

"Your father and I will make that judgment, Caitlin. Sonia seems harmless enough, and it's good for Pegasus to make friends with many different kinds of people. I must say her level of compassion seems a whole lot higher than yours." Mommy's voice turned into stone. "Sonia is a suitable-aged friend for you, Caitlin. Since you're so concerned about the friends your little sister makes, why don't you and Brandi take over for her?"

"Really, Mother. You're just impossible. That Sonia is so gross. She shuffles around like this zombie or something, with her head down and her mouth hanging open and drooling and... I mean, Brandi and those guys would just... Besides, what if Mr. Emmett saw her?"

"He'd like her," I said then, hopping with both feets into the kitchen. I talked fast before Mommy could yell at Caitlin, *Where is your human consideration?* She always yells that about this time, her voice an invisible knife that sounds like it's slashing Caitlin's ears in half. (I don't like hearing knives, even when they're invisible ones and headed for Caitlin stead of me.)

"He'd like her better than you and me together," I went on. "Mr. Emmett gots four eyes, Caitlin, same as Peter. I know now what that means—they both wear glasses. Is Mr. Emmett also a four-eyed nerd?"

"Certainly not! Mr. Emmett has two college degrees, the same as Daddy. He once played for a symphony orchestra. He is a Man of Distinction."

I knew she would say that. A Man of Stinking is Caitlin's special name for Mr. Emmett. "He is not a Man of Stinking," I argued. "He is your Secret Sweetheart." And then I sang, "Caitlin loves Mr. Emmett. Caitlin loves Mr. Emmett. . . ." Over and over and over.

Caitlin screamed and chased me into the living room, where I turned me into a snake wearing a knee sock on her tail. Mommy yelled at both of us. But she only yelled, "Be careful! Cut it out!" I think I made her forget to yell, *Where is your human consideration?*

But today she does yell that.

Only this time she yells it not at Caitlin, but at *me*.

She yells it after me and Sonia plog through the front door. Because I'm one whole hour late for my piano lesson.

Actually, she doesn't yell that first. "Margaret Elizabeth!" She says that first, shaking me with tears striping her cheeks. "Where have you been all this time? Are you all *right?*"

"Yes, but 'cept for feeling shaked like Jell-O." I wriggle hard inside her arms, then smile when her fingers let go my shoulders to wipe her eyes. "That's better, Mommy. Why are you crying, though? Are *you* all right?"

"Margaret, I was worried sick! You come home an hour late from school. First Alan bursts in with some story about a gang of bullies chasing you both home, but you're not with him and he can't even tell me where you are. . . . What happened, baby? Did those bad boys hurt you?"

"No, Mommy. They only waggled sticks at me, but you know what? I turned me into a lion with claws and pointy teeth." I feel all glowy-proud when I tell my story. "That lion scared them stickless! She scared them so bad they turned into rats and birds, like what Motorthroat eats."

"Peggy say, 'Grrr.' " Sonia smiles big at Mommy, turns her own hands into pretend claws. "Her go like this—"

But Mommy interrupts. "How dare you?" she yells, but at me—not at Sonia. Then she says it. "Margaret Elizabeth Kendall! Where is your human consideration?"

A stone plunks in my middle. I freeze when I stare up at Mommy, at her eyes like flashing pins and her face the color of tomato juice. "It's inside me, like the lion," I answer bravely. "I am not like Caitlin. Me and Sonia—"

"Were playing a pointless make-believe game." Mommy interrupts me this time. "Here I am worried sick, about to send out a search party, and here comes poor Mr. Emmett for your piano lesson—and waits for you an hour! And then he has to leave because he's due to give another lesson, but first he offers to go combing the neighborhood for you. . . . And all this time," she asks, "you were pretending to be a lion?"

"They thought the lion was real, Mommy! Those boys-poys ran away from her, but 'cept then they turned into rats and birds."

"So you made this whole thing up. I must say you disappoint me, young lady." Her pin-eyes flash at Sonia. "You! I'm taking you straight back to your own house, soon as I deal with Margaret here. I don't want you following her home anymore."

"Grrr!" That is me, not Sonia. She just sags and stares down cave-mouthed at the floor.

I turn into the lion again. This time she pounces at Mommy—and Mommy is the rat. But cept Mommy doesn't run away. Instead, she grabs me and spins me round and spanks the lion gone. Then she sends me upstairs to my room, just like those times when I was rude to Mrs. Winthrop.

"I hate you, Mommy!" I tell my pillow, stomping it with both my feets. "When you come in this time I won't talk to you or even let you sit me on your lap. I'll just

Ignore you, like what Alan does to those mean ol' boys-poys...."

Knock-knock.

"May I come in?" The voice is not Mommy's, but Alan's. So I say yes.

Alan plunks down on my bed and breathes a branch-long wind. He doesn't pull me onto his lap like Mommy would, he only sits real quiet then finally looks at me. Tears sparkle like raindrops on the leaves that are his eyes. "I'm sorry, Pegasus," he says in his mumble-voice. "I'm sorry I didn't stay to protect you from those boys. Did you really chase them gone all by yourself?"

"No, the lion did. But that ol' Mommy-pommy won't believe me." I kick my pillow across the rug, feeling hot rain splash down from my own eyes. "She yelled at Sonia, too. She told her not to follow me home anymore...." A throat stone bangs dead my talking. I cry instead.

"I ... I let you guys get in trouble." Alan also cries, rolling his fingers into stones and hammering his knees. "I'm a coward! A scaredy-cat! I really am a Bug Brain, just like Mitchell Brannon says."

"He's a Bird-Rat Fortissimo!"

Alan doesn't seem to hear me. "I don't mean to be a coward," he goes on. "But whenever he yells stuff at me or punches me, I just want to disappear. My stomach feels all knotted up inside. My knees turn to Jell-O—not literally, of course." He smiles at my smile, then switches to sad again. "And I can't even stick up for somebody else who is different—or even for my own little sister. Even you, Pegasus—even *you* stood up to those bullies. And you're still just a little kid!"

I'm in third grade same as you, I would argue usually. But now Alan looks too saggy-sad for arguing. "It wasn't really me who made them scared," I say instead. "I told the truth to Mommy. It was actually the lion."

I wait for him to say, *That is not logical. Lions live only at the zoo or in the African rainforests.* But he doesn't. Instead, he observes me interested. "What lion do you mean, Pegasus?"

"The one who lives inside me," I explain. "She is not like me, 'cause I am usually a scaredy-cat too. But today I felt so mad she jumped right out of me—and those boys never knew she was pretend." I think of something. "You know what, Alan? Maybe you also got an animal inside you! What is the meanest kind you know?"

"A shark. No, a cobra. Or maybe a crocodile." Alan frowns, wiping his eyes with his fingers. Suddenly he smiles all sparkly at me. His eye-leaves shine with sun instead of rain. "That's an excellent theory, Pegasus. You think it would also work for me?"

"Yes. I think a shark would *really* make him run, that mean ol' Mitchell!" We burst out laughing when we think of this together—so hard we forget to feel mad or saggy-sad. And we don't even mind when Mommy steps through my bedroom door.

She plops down on my bed and pulls us both onto her lap, even though usually she says Alan is too big. She hugs us both. Then she looks at me all rainy-eyed, her hand gently pushing back my forehead-hairs.

"Oh, Pegasus. I'm so sorry I got mad and didn't believe you." She shakes her head. "Your daddy just called me. He noticed you on the way to his publisher's. And he said he saw the whole thing—those boys tormenting you and Sonia, then turning tail and fleeing—without you laying a hand on one of them."

"Yes. I only laid *grrrr's* on them, plus pretend pointy teeth and claws."

This time Mommy smiles an Alan-smile. "Daddy started to get out and help you two, but then he saw those boys back off and run away from you. He does plan to talk with your teacher and the boys' parents, though, because those kids have no business acting like big bullies." Her eyes again turn rainy. "Can you forgive me, Pegasus?"

"Yes, Mommy. Will you forgive Sonia, too?"

"Sonia too," Mommy promises, then smiles at Alan. "There's no real shame in being different, son," she tells him. "You and Pegasus are both very special in different ways. You'll find your own kind of courage." She pushes us off her lap. "Off with you both now, to play while I get supper. Sonia's still here, you know. I called her mother, and she said there still is plenty of time for her to stay and play with you."

So we race downstairs to play with Sonia—me and Alan both.

12.

A DIFFERENT KIND OF COURAGE

Sonia is my new best friend.

We play together every day at recess. We play on the swings and slide and even the jungle gym, though on there we haven't climbed yet above the bottom rung. "Sissies!" Mitchell Brannon yells—but safely from the bench with Mrs. Stone.

Now *he* is the one who sits and observes instead—whenever Mrs. Stone catches him being a bully. Plus, he also takes off for that bench whenever he sees me start to turn into the lion. I do this every time he heads for Sonia with some sticks or mud. And I think he is finally giving up.

These days, I like to turn me into many things—a lion, a purple cloud, a horse with wings, a one-socked snake. Sometimes me and Sonia both turn into Martians with ten red eyes. Sonia likes to always be the same things as me. She follows me everywhere, doing whatever I do only more.

Sometimes she follows Alan too, Alan when he teaches her the names of bugs and stones. He lets her hold his magnifying glass. "Mica. June bug. Graphite. Praying mantis." He says the names real slow for her. She speaks them after him, blurrier but getting them all right. "Correct, Sonia!" Alan smiles with sparkles in his eyes. Sonia laughs and claps and drops the magnifying glass. But that's okay, cause it's make from a thick kind of glass that doesn't break.

One day Mitchell Brannon tries to break it on purpose. He does this right after the first time I roar him to the bench. "Ha-ha, scared you!" I call after him.

He bounces back up and stretches his arms, pretends to yawn. "Naw, you didn't," he argues. "I ain't scared of no dorky little girls." But even so, he keeps away from me and Sonia both. Instead, he darts up to Alan and grabs his magnifying glass. He throws it *bang* against a monkey bar.

I stand there feeling freezed, remembering Alan doesn't like me to protect him. Then I also remember our talking in my room, that day after my mad-lion jumped out and chased Mitchell away. Maybe Alan's animal inside will jump out, I think now. I wonder what kind of animal he will be. A shark? A cobra? Or maybe a crocodile?

But Alan just stands there being Alan. This time, though, he doesn't tremble. And he also doesn't slink off with his face the color of tomato juice. Instead, he stares at Mitchell's face about a million years. At last he smiles and says in a glowy-proud voice, "Great throw, Mitchell! That was an excellent hit."

Mitchell looks surprised for a minute. Then his face twists back into its snarl. "You think you're so smart!" he yells. "You with your fancy bugs' names an' your hundred on Old Stoneface's stupid math quiz! Well, I don't like nerds who act smarter'n me. I don't like how you creeps get all the attention." He rolls his fingers into stones and makes a pretend punch. "Whatcha gonna do about it, Bug Brain?"

Alan doesn't cry or jump backwards from the punch. He frowns at Mitchell's hand-stones with his thinking face on. "I won't fight you, Mitchell," he says at last, real calm. "I know you would win, 'cause you're smarter than me at punching people out. You're also smarter than me at catching and throwing balls and climbing ropes." He smiles again. "I think you can even read a little better than me. You are actually smarter than me in many ways."

Mitchell's snarling mouth and eyes turn slowly into circles. He drops his hand-stones, which unroll back into just fingers. "Yeah?" he asks real soft, after another million years. "You really think so, man?"

"Sure, Mitchell." Alan spreads his smile even bigger and more sparkly. "Hey, you want to make a deal?"

"What deal?" Mitchell frowns at him again.

"You teach me how to throw and catch and hit things with a ball. Then I'll teach you how to add numbers inside your head. It's a really cool trick, and it'll help you get an A on the next math quiz. Plus, it will be our special secret. Okay, Mitchell?"

"Okay Alan!" This is the first time Mitchell calls my brother by his real name. He smiles unmeanly too. His real smile make his freckles look like dancing stead of snarling. Then he slaps Alan's inside hands—but cept not hard this time, the way he does that usually. The two of them race off like real best friends, flapping their arms and making airplane sounds.

"I did it, Pegasus!" Alan laughs and cheers after school, arm-flapping and airplaning round me. "I actually hit the backboard with Mitchell's ball. Plus, I caught it by myself afterwards."

"You also made friends with that mean ol' Mitchell Brannon. But 'cept now he is nice instead of mean."

"That's true, Pegasus—'specially after he learned the number trick I taught him during math. He did all the problems I gave him correctly, too. Man, was he proud!" Alan observes his fingers and talks more quiet now. "I think it's like what Daddy said when he came home after talking to Mrs. Stone and Mitchell's dad. He found out Mitchell's mom died only last year in a car wreck, and his dad works a lot and doesn't have time to pay him much attention. So he said maybe Mitchell acts mean 'cause he feels insecure inside."

"What is insecure?"

"That means how we feel sometimes, dumb and not too special. And he said when we acted scared of Mitchell, it prob'ly made him feel a little smarter."

"But now he doesn't got to, 'cause you proved to him he really *is* smart. Plus, you didn't even have to use your animal inside." I think and remember something else. "Alan, was that what Mommy meant when she talked about your different kind of courage?"

"Maybe." Alan smiles down at a dragonfly on his hands, and his face turns pink again like my seashell. "Anyways, I don't got to feel scared anymore—'specially since Mitchell is my friend."

"And your tutor, too," I remind him. "Not the kind that toots on flutes, but the other kind that Mrs. Stone explained us. I think you are also Mitchell's tutor."

"Yeah. I guess we're sort of tutors for each other." Alan makes another airplane-spin. "Hey, Pegasus!"

"What?" I ask him, spinning too.

"Let's also go ahead and tutor Sonia! Let's tell Mrs. Stone we'll do it after all."

And this is exactly what we do.

13.

TUTORS AND GENIUSES

Our tutoring times with Sonia are three days after school, the afternoons when we don't got piano lessons. On those days after class, we all walk to the Resource Room. This is a little room the same as Register, but cept with tables inside stead of a desk or a long hard board.

We all sit round one table, me and Alan and Sonia with our books and papers and pencils and our letter and number cards. And we put our heads together—in what Daddy said are more ways than one.

Actually, almost all of us are tutors for each other. I help Alan understand the bugs that are words on paper. He already knows a lot of them, almost as many as realife bugs. But sometimes he sees the word-bugs and their letters turned round backwards.

Alan helps me understand those bugs that make 2+2 and tables. I mean the tables with x's in, not the flat and woody kind we sit at.

And both of us help Sonia, Alan with counting ten number-bugs and me with learning all the letter ones.

Only Sonia is not anyone's tutor. She's a trier instead—at least until the roof part of her A zigs off the paper. Then she groans and punches her head and shoves her paper at me. "You do it, Peggy."

"No, Sonia." I shove her paper back. "You can do it yourself. Just try."

Then Sonia tries with all of herself. Her mouth pumps out hard wind, and her tongue curls up and presses against her nose. But all her trying never seems to work.

Is Sonia really dumb? I wonder sometimes. Everybody else thinks that. The grown-ups shake their heads at her with cloudy faces—even Mommy and Daddy and Mrs. Stone. Caitlin looks at her like she is one of Alan's bugs. And the kids at school still stare at her with mean-mud in their eyes—even though they no longer throw that mud.

At recess now I sometimes play with Ashley and Danielle. We pretend to be horses with wings and forehead-horns. But even they don't like it when Sonia joins our games. "She's such a drag, Pegasus. She never understands anything."

And then Haley.

The next time I see Haley, walking home from school, she darts across the street soon as she sees I am with Sonia. "I'll see you by yourself, Margaret-pargaret," she yells from the other side. "But I'm not walking with any ol' Dummy Head!"

"Sonia is not a Dummy Head," I argue. "She is a Sonia Head."

"Same thing." Haley snorts a Caitlin-Brandi snort.

"I don't think so." I answer her the same way Alan would. "I can hear the difference 'tween them. It's obvious."

"You're crazy, Margaret Kendall!" Haley yells again. "Anyways, I'd rather walk home with Brittany and Sarah. I like them better than you now." She skips ahead to join her two new friends, the ones she made in her kidney-garden class. I watch their skipping backs turn all blurry through my tears. And a big gray stone plunks down into my chest.

Does Sonia, I wonder, feel that chest-stone all the time?

How does it feel to be worst at *everything?*

One day Sonia tries so hard her pencil point snaps off. "I'll go sharpen it," I say, and I jump up from my chair. But then I trip over something and almost tumble forward to the floor. I catch myself on a table corner and frown down at the something.

It's actually four somethings. The same ones that always make me trip.

"Old string-worms!" I yell down at my running shoes. "They escaped again!"

"Here, Pegasus," Alan says. "Let me tie them for you."

"No, Alan." Sonia says that. And she sounds, for the first time ever, almost bossy like Caitlin. "Peggy do that herself. Just like Sonia."

"But Sonia, I don't know how yet," I explain to her.

"Peggy try."

So I do.

Like always, those old shoestrings get all tangled up inside my stubborn fingers. Like always, they only make spaghettis. But this time I don't stop after the first try. I listen real hard to Alan's slow directions. I also listen to Sonia saying, "Try. Try again." Over and over.

My fingers listen too.

And at last they make a worm-knot—and then a wobbly bow!

"I did it!" I feel sparkly inside. "Look, Alan! Look, Sonia! I can tie my own shoes, same as you guys!"

Alan cheers me now, but Sonia's face-sun slips behind a cloud. When I hand her the sharpened pencil, she just drops it in her lap. Then she sobs and slumps over forward.

"What's the matter, Sonia?" I pet her back, which feels all trembly.

"I can't tie shoes," she explains to her chest in a choky voice. "Peggy try—yes. Sonia try—no!" She shakes her head and wipes her tear-wet eyes with her fingers. She sniffles, blows her nose on those fingers, then rubs the nose stuff off against her paper. "Sonia can't do nothing," she goes on. "It 'cause I a retard. That means dumb."

A big stone plunks inside my chest, chasing gone the sparkly.

"No, it doesn't, Sonia," Alan argues. *"Retard* actually means to make slow—like the way I have to read words. But I won't call you that anyways, 'cause it's not a cool word to use for people."

"Retard is a word you're s'posed to use only for music," I tell her. Actually, I remember the music word is a little different. But it sounds almost the same, only nicer.

"Music?" Sonia asks. Her smile drifts back onto her face—like sunshine bursting out from behind the cloud. She lifts her head and laughs then and claps her sticky hands. "I like music, Peggy!"

And that is what gives me a super cool idea.

The next day is not tutoring, but my piano lesson with Mr. Emmett. There I am not a tutor, but a trier same as Sonia. I'm the worst trier, too! If Sonia comes home with me then, I think, she could watch me miss my fingering. She could laugh when Mr. Emmett washes his hands at my mistakes. Then she would know she is not the only one who is worst at everything.

So that afternoon I invite Sonia to walk home from school with me. Even though it's a day for my piano lesson.

Caitlin opens the door when we get home. She stares at me and Sonia both with nails in her eyes. "Pegasus," she says hissing, like Sonia cannot hear. "You're not dragging *her* in here, I hope. Mr. Emmett is here for your piano lesson. I'll be simply *mortified* if he sees you with your cross-eyed—"

"Caitlin!" Mommy interrupts right behind her like a knife. "That's enough! Go to your room at once, and wait for me in there."

"You're not cross-eyed, Sonia," I comfort her. "Your eyes just swim up closer to your nose than ours do." I turn to ask Mommy a question. "If your eyes fell into your nose, could you see yourself breathing?"

Mommy doesn't answer me. She's too busy watching with angry hands on hips while Caitlin stomps hard-breathing up the stairs. She shakes her head, then tells me to hurry in for my piano lesson. Then she smiles at Sonia like rainy sunshine. "You're always welcome here, honey. Just be sure to listen quietly while Pegasus has her lesson. And I'd better call your mother to let her know you're here."

"Don't mind Caitlin, Sonia." I comfort her some more when we plog into the living room. "She is blue-skin-eyed, and you know what she calls Mr. Emmett? A—"

"Greetings, Pegasus." Mr. Emmett interrupts me, before I can finish my sentence: "Man of Stinking." He is not Stinking, only trembling and smiling the way he usually does. He stands up from his chair and steps over to us both, holding out one milky hand to Sonia. He looks at her with questions in his eyes. "Is this a new student?"

"This is Sonia," I tell him proudly. "She is my best friend and also my student. But today she wanted to come and watch *me* be the student instead."

"I'm enchanted, Sonia." Mr. Emmett takes her hand, then bows to her. He smiles at her like sunshine with no rain, so I know *enchanted* does not mean the same as *mortified.*

But when I play my scales, he does look mortified. "Watch your fingering, dear child." He shivers on the bench. "You must pay attention!"

So I try, but still my fingers do Something Else Again. The music jumping out is also Something Else Again.

"Now *you* play one, Mr. Emmett," I beg him at last. "Play the song that sounds like a cloud tripping over the sun. The one where he skins his cloud-knees and they bleed into the water."

Mr. Emmett shakes his head at me and groans. "I'll play it for you afterwards, my dear," he promises. "You know our lesson must come first." He looks over at Sonia then and laughs, and Sonia laughs along with him from the fat green chair. "Our Pegasus here is certainly a born writer," he tells her. "A born actress, too, from what I've heard. But will we ever make a musician out of her?"

"Okay," I answer him, when Sonia only smiles. "But first I got to go to the bathroom."

I really do, too. But after flushing I scoop up Motorthroat, to stop her from drinking out the toilet. I hug her purring body, rubbing the stiff from my fingers off onto her stripy fur. Then I dance with her awhile. She is a lion in a story I just wrote. Next we both turn into real live actresses on a stage, and the stage is also in my story. . . .

Then comes music for our dancing.

It swims upstairs from the living room. It's my favorite Mr. Emmett song, the one about the cloud bleeding rosy evening sunshine into water. I quick dart out the bathroom and race downstairs, back into the living room. Motorthroat jumps out my arms and dives beneath the sofa. I think she feels surprised as me by what we see.

Sonia is playing the piano!

Mr. Emmett watches her play. He's not sitting beside her on the bench, frowning and telling her to watch her fingering. Instead, he's plopped down now in the same fat green chair where Sonia sat before. He's watching her the same way people always watch *him* play. And Mommy and Caitlin, on the sofa, watch her that way too.

None of them looks sad or head-shaking or mortified. Instead, they wear what me and Alan call the Genius Face. It is how grown-ups look when I first read to them out loud. Or when Alan does some super-smart number tricks inside his head.

Sonia looks like a glowing sunrise. I can tell this is one time she doesn't feel that stone inside her chest. When she plays Mr. Emmett's special song, she crashes out all its blood and light and complicated dreams. Plus, she doesn't make even one mistake.

"Phenomenal," Mr. Emmett says afterwards. "The child claims she's never had lessons." Like me with my reading, I think smiling. And like Alan with his secret number tricks. Some things just come easy to us all. But other things are always lots more hard.

I look down at my running shoes, tied for the first time by myself just yesterday. Sonia helped me do that, I remember. If she didn't make me try I would probly still not know how. She really is my tutor, after all! All three of us—Alan and Sonia and me—are tutors for each other.

The next day I write in my Composition:

God made everybody different but not dumb. I observed that my friend Sonia is a genius three.

14.

A NOBLE DEED

"What are you supposed to be?" Caitlin wrinkles her nose at me. "Pegasus the Pest?"

"I am not a pest," I tell her. "I'm a lionorse. I made that word myself. It means a cross between—"

"Spare me. And what're *you,* Twerp?" She turns her glare to Alan, who stands right next to me in his sheet of crookedy holes. Between those holes are crayoned lots of red and squiggly dots. A long rip shaped like lightning zig-zags all down his front.

"A cell nucleus." Alan grins at Caitlin through the rip and shakes his head. "I wanted it to look accurate, as seen from a microscope. But unfortunately"—he dips his head—"my scissors slipped a little."

"A lot, I'd say." Caitlin groans. "Why can't you kids be something normal, like ghosts or witches?"

Mommy steps into the living room and answers for us. "Because we wanted them to be something from their own imaginations." She smiles at our costumes. "Something that honors the Lord."

Daddy strides in right behind her, smiling too. "Our family wants to stand for good instead of evil," he explains. "They're using this night to perform a noble deed."

The paper bags we carry are not for candy, but instead for money to buy food for starving children. "Mrs. Winthrop will give us candy anyways," Alan tells me.

"Cool, Alan!" I spin around in circles. "But let's save part of that for the children too—in case the money just buys them vegetables."

Mommy and Daddy both smile when Alan says okay. But Caitlin makes a vegetable-eating face. She is in a stinky mood cause of Brandi's party. She wants to go to that, but Mommy and Daddy both said Absolutely Not. "Especially not after that fiasco here last summer," Mommy goes on now. "We just don't think Brandi and her friends can be trusted. Besides, you already promised to take Alan and Pegasus round for Trick-or-Treat."

Caitlin starts to argue, but then the doorbell dings.

I run to open it and let in a woody box. The box looks Caitlin-sized, long and square and filled with ziggy doors like the ones on Dileth's maze. "Hello," it says in a Peter-voice, soft with wind. Then out from one of its doors pops a marshmallow with fur and a mousy face.

"Dileth!" I cheer, clapping my hands.

"Cool!" Alan claps too. "You're Peter! You're Dileth's maze!"

"Quite an impressive costume, Peter." Daddy says that, and Mommy nods with him as they smile at Peter's box. But Caitlin only rolls her blue-skinned eyes at the ceiling.

The woody box with Peter inside walks straight over to her. "Uh, Caitlin?" it says, its Peter-voice filled with even more wind than usually. "Can I go with you to take Alan and Pegasus round the neighborhood?"

"Certainly not." Caitlin talks not to Peter's box, but to the ceiling. "Do you intend to socially embarrass me for life? I'm not about to go traipsing around town in the company of *three mere children.*"

"*Caitlin!*" Daddy roars like a lion. "You'll take the kids. You'll go with Peter. Understand?"

"Yes, Daddy." She answers him like one of Dileth's squeaks. I smile when I pull on my lionorse head—a crayon-faced grocery bag with pointy ears and teeth and holes for eyes. Caitlin's eyes stab holes in all of us. But she

A NOBLE DEED

grabs our hands anyways and drags us out the door. The box filled with Peter and Dileth clumps behind.

Outside is filled with chirps of crickets and kids barfed out from cars. Soft wind swims through the black tree-bones, stirs the crunchy ground-leaves round in circles. The kids also stir those leaves, crunching up to houses that got smiling pumpkins in their windows. One of those windows is Mrs. Winthrop's, and one of those kids is Haley in her Strawberry Shortcake dress. I try to skip ahead, but Caitlin's hand pulls fire through my arm. "Wait," she says in her bossy voice. "I need to talk to Peter first. Okay?"

So we wait while she asks him will he take us by himself. "I really need to study at the library for a test." (That is a lie, but I know better than to say this when she's in a stinky mood.) "You guys can meet me there at nine when you're done," she goes on. "We'll all walk home together, and that way my parents will never know the difference. Okay, Peter? Do this for me, and I promise to be your project partner at the Science Fair."

"I don't know, Caitlin . . ."

She starts to argue, but a roaring monster interrupts. This monster is not a costume with a little kid inside. He is Caitlin's boyfriend Hairy Barry, with a Moped under his legs.

The Moped part of the monster stops his roaring. The Hairy Barry part flashes us his sharky smile. "Hey, you turkeys," he says, in his voice that gots even more snarl than Caitlin's.

I argue, "We are not turkeys. I'm a lionorse, and Alan is—"

"Hey, Cat Girl!" Barry interrupts, grinning at Caitlin. "I heard Brandi's bash is like totally gnarly! Wanna go?"

"Okay, Barry." Caitlin smiles at him, lets go our hands. "But I absolutely have to leave there at a quarter to nine." She climbs up on the Moped, right behind Harry Barry. "See you guys," she calls out when the roaring starts up again. She sounds real happy now. "At the library. At nine. Remember!" The monster roars louder and eats up all her voice. Then it roars her gone down the street.

"Man, will Caitlin be in trouble." Alan shakes his head.

"I don't care." I rub her yanking fire from my arm. "She likes old Hairy Barry better than us. Anyways, we'll have more fun by ourselves. Right, Peter?" I grab one hand from Peter's box and dance it round in happy circles.

But Peter in his box does not act happy. He just stands there looking freezed and staring down the street. "Was that guy Barry Bruner?"

"Yes," I say. "But me and Alan call him Hairy Barry. He is actually a bark, which means a cross between a bear and a—"

"Come on. Let's go," Peter interrupts. "We got to get her away from him. Now!" His voice crackles like popcorn, then jumps high with squeaky-scared. He grabs our hands and starts to run, dragging me and Alan along with him. "I heard about that guy," he says to us between his hard breathing. "He's like really bad. I ... I heard he got this one girl into trouble."

"Caitlin will *really* be in trouble," Alan says.

I ask, "What kind of trouble? Did he dare her to stick a snake in the shower?" I dared Alan to do that once when company stayed overnight. Mommy spanked both of us the same.

Peter doesn't answer me. Instead he asks, "Where does Brandi live?" We tell him, and he drags us even faster. By the time we reach her street, we are all breathing much too hard to talk.

We can hear Brandi's house even before we see it. That music like a chainy fence is screaming an entire block away. We all cover our ears when we reach Brandi's front porch.

"Maybe you kids better wait out here," Peter says, looking all worried. But when he slips into the house, we follow right behind him.

The living room is filled with Caitlin-sized peoples, all laughing and talking and jumping up and down. Some of them are smoking cigarettes, ones that make sour blue smoke swim up my nose. Others are drinking golden juice inside fat cups with skinny stems. It looks like in our living room last summer when we sneaked to Mrs. Winthrop's. But cept it's smokier and even louder.

We sneak through the smoky holes between the peoples, pushing past more boys who got bald heads with giant toothbrushes on top. This time I don't feel like laughing at them, though. Caitlin will be mad at us, I think shivering. If Mommy and Daddy ground her, she'll act mean to us forever. Plus, she'll never-ever be friends with Peter—

"Barry, *no!* That's *gross!* I thought we were just friends. I can't *believe* you want us to—"

"Aw, c'mon, Cat Girl. It'll be fun—"

"*Stop* it, Barry! Let me *go!* I don't *want* to go in there!"

We hear them first, then see them.

Caitlin does not look happy anymore. Her face is streaked bright red from scared and mad, but I think she's mad at Barry stead of us. They're fighting like those wrestlers on TV, but cept Hairy Barry still gots on his sharky smile. One of his stony hands yanks at Caitlin's arm, while the other hand pushes at a half-open door.

Peter leaps between them, like a sudden blur. He reaches inside one of the doors on his box and pulls out

Dileth. Then he dumps his white rat smack on top of Harry Barry's head.

Barry screams, lets go Caitlin's arm. He jumps backwards with a scared face that wrinkles into mad. And he spits a funny word I never heard before, but it sounds mean like those names Mitchell Brannon used to call us.

"Peter!" Caitlin yells. But she does not act mad at him or even roll her eyes. Instead, she throws her arms around his box. "Let's get out of here."

Peter snatches Dileth off old Barry's head, pokes him back through the door on his box. Then he grabs Caitlin's hand, and we all start running. (All but cept for Hairy Barry, who just stands there snarling funny words.) We charge through all those peoples and that blue smoke and chainy-fence music. Out Brandi's door and down the street.

Caitlin cries against Peter's box the whole way home. "Oh, Peter," she says in a choky voice between her sobbing. "I'm so glad you guys came and rescued me."

"Really?" Peter's voice pops again, jumps up high like Dileth's squeak.

"Of course, you goofball." Caitlin smiles at his box like rainy sunshine, but then she's crying once again. "Oh, it was so horrible! I never dreamed that total creep would try to . . . Maybe it was just that he had too much to drink. I mean, I promise he never acted that way to me before."

"What did he try to do, Caitlin?" Me and Alan both ask that at once, but she doesn't answer.

"Did he make you drink weed killer?" Alan guesses.

"Or cut you up into fifty zillion pieces?" I ask that.

Caitlin doesn't answer us, of course. And Peter ignores us too. "I believe you, Caitlin," he says in his quiet voice. "Are you sure he didn't hurt you, though?"

"Only to make me positively mortified."

"It's okay, Caitlin. We're almost at your house. You'll feel better when you tell your mom and dad."

Caitlin makes a barfing sound when he says that, and me and Alan just look at each other. When Mommy and Daddy open the front door, they're both smiling like the pumpkin in our window. "Whatever are you kids doing home so early?" Mommy sounds surprised. "It's not even eight-thirty yet."

We wait for Caitlin to tell one of her interesting lies—the one about her library test, or maybe that Mrs. Winthrop's taffy made her barf for real. But she doesn't. Instead, she turns herself into a wet and wailing hug around them both.

"Mommy! Daddy!" She says that like me and Alan do when we skin our knees (that's me) or break our collar bones (that's Alan, when he fell out the elm tree twice). "Please forgive me! No, don't. Ground me. Ground me for a year, 'cause I deserve it. Only I promise I'll never, ever do it again."

And then she tells them exactly what she did.

Actually, she doesn't talk clear enough for me to understand. Her voice breaks into a splintered glass with all its water spilled out. Mommy and Daddy have to walk her inside, circling her between their hugs as they head for the kitchen. But even in there no yelling bursts out when Peter follows them, or when me and Alan listen by the door. Only a few more Caitlin-sobs, then talking like soft hums.

At last Daddy and Peter come back out to the living room. Daddy breathes a tired wind, looking sad but smiling at the same time. "Well, troops," he says at last. "I hardly know what to say."

"I'm sorry, Mr. Kendall." Peter steps his box backwards, washing his hands without soap. "About the kids, I mean. I know I was wrong to let them follow me into that house. And I guess I should've called you from there to come pick them up. Prob'ly would've still had time to come back and take them round for Trick-or-Treat later on. Well, at least if I had my dad's car. Except I don't know how to drive it yet...."

Daddy claps a corner of his box. "You might have used a little better judgment this time, Peter. But you do know how to be a friend. A far better friend to Caitlin than she's recently deserved."

Suddenly I stare down at the empty inside my bag. The empty there instead of money or candy from Mrs. Winthrop. "Daddy!" I shout, feeling freezed inside. "We were so busy rescuing Caitlin we forgot to perform our noble deed!"

"Easy there, Pegasus, my love." Daddy pulls all three of us into a smiling hug. "We'll collect donations for the kids tomorrow. For tonight, you young scamps performed a sufficient noble deed."

15.

CHANGES

Caitlin is like a different person now.

    She no longer wobbles on pointy heels or paints her eyeskins blue. She twists her hairs, which are growing long, into carrots same as mine (but cept colored sand instead of orange). She even plays with us sometimes—not just piano but also pretend games, like being E.T. or a princess from my book of fairy tales.

    Mommy and Daddy did not ground Caitlin for going that night to Brandi's party. "It sounds like you learned your lesson and were punished quite enough already," Mommy said. But Caitlin grounded herself anyways. At night she now stays home and reads instead of telling lies and sneaking out. And the only friend she calls on the phone is Peter.

    "Whatever happened to Brandi?" Mommy asks her one day. She sounds more happy in her wondering than worried.

    "Who even knows?" Caitlin flips back her sandy-colored hair-carrots and breathes soft wind. "That old Brandi thinks she's so grown up. Mom, she actually told me she thinks it's okay to—you know—with a boy." Caitlin shivers hard. "I told her I'm sick of all that crud. We're only fourteen, after all. I've had it with Barry Bruner and all those creeps, and I think she's really crazy to hang out with them. Besides, I know she wouldn't understand about Peter."

    But me and Alan understand, and we turn into laughing airplanes whenever we think of it. Since that night we rescued her, Caitlin's let Peter be her boyfriend!

On the phone to him she talks about not boys, but his science project. They are finally working on that together. Caitlin does the reading part and Peter the Dileth part. Dileth has to run his maze in the same room as Caitlin, but even so she never screams or jumps on chairs. She's never screamed from Dileth even once, but cept for that night when he got dumped on top old Harry Barry's head. "And for that time," she told Peter, "I owe your beast forever some common courtesy. He helped rescue me from a fate worse than death."

"What fate?" Me and Alan ask her that whenever we remember. "What did Harry Barry try to do?" We make this a guessing game, like Twenty Questions.

"Did he try to flush you down the toilet?"

"Or hang you up on the bedroom door by your toenails?"

"Or make you drink stinky medicine that would turn you into a purple frog?"

But Caitlin never will answer us, even now. "Questions, questions!" She says that groaning, same as she always did. And she still stares at us with nails in her eyes. "Can't you little pests see when a person would rather not talk about something?"

We shake our heads as we watch her stomp away breathing hard. "I guess in some ways," Alan observes, "people never change."

"I hope Peter never changes," I tell him day when he says that. "Let's go ask him about what happened that night. He will tell us, Alan."

But he doesn't. Peter's busy switching round some doors on Dileth's maze. He bends his head with Caitlin's over the page she's reading from his book. He frowns when she reads, thinking hard and ignoring Alan's question. And at last when we both ask it three times each, he looks up and frowns at us instead. "Look, you two," he says, grinding the words like stones between his teeth. "It's really not worth knowing. So please quit asking that, okay?"

"Okay, Peter," Alan says, the sparkly gone from his voice. "I'll help you change the pattern of Dileth's maze. Are you making a more complicated one? Do you think he'll be smart enough to learn it?"

"I'll tutor him," I say, patting his head. "He'll learn it the same way I learned to tie my shoes. Let's teach Dileth also how to tie a bow."

"That's not logical, Pegasus," Alan argues. "The purpose of this project is to focus on him learning just the maze. Right, Peter? Or is her theory possible? Can a white rat learn to run mazes and tie bows at the same time? Can we help teach—"

"Shut up!" Caitlin yells, holding her ears. "Make them go away, Peter. They're giving me a headache."

We ignore her, wait for Peter to answer our interesting questions. But his frown stays sticked onto his oatmeal face. "You kids better go," he says instead. "Me and Caitlin are busy working on our project now."

"But Peter, it's *all* our project," I argue. "We're all s'posed to work on it together!"

Alan says nothing. He only grabs my hand and walks me fast to the door. "Come on, Pegasus. They don't want us here anymore. Peter likes Caitlin now better than us."

Alan won't talk to me outside. His face swims with milk and then tomato juice. The leaves that are his eyes look filled with rain. He wipes those eyes with his fingers and does not let me comfort him. Instead, he darts off down the street to play with his new friend Mitchell Brannon.

I hop after him, practicing on only one foot.

"Whatcha wanna hang out with him for, anyways?" Mitchell asks when Alan complains to him about Peter. "My brother Jeff, who's in high school with him, says he's just a total nerd."

"My sister Caitlin used to say that too. But now she hangs out with him all the time. Peter is *her* best friend instead of mine."

"Yeah?" Mitchell laughs. "Well then, she must be a total nerd too. Jeff says—"

But right then Alan jumps on Mitchell and locks him in a hug. It's the kind of angry hug that squeezes gone your talking, that makes you fall down backwards to the ground. I never saw Alan hug that way before.

"Hey, Alan! I take it back about your sister!" Mitchell sounds all squeaky like Dileth. He's flopping around on the grass beneath my brother, who traps him like a cage. But he only grins when Alan lets him go. "Hey, man," he says, scrambling up and play-punching at Alan's shoulders. "You're getting pretty good!"

"That wasn't me, Mitchell. It was a boa constrictor." Alan grins back at him, forgetting to act mad. "They actually do that, you know. They hug their prey hard enough to squeeze it to death. That's a scientific fact."

"No kidding, man? How's about rattlesnakes?" Mitchell sounds really interested. He and Alan both turn into talking airplanes, forgetting to feel mad or saggy-sad.

They also both forget I'm even there.

I guess everybody changes but cept me, I think sadly. A lonely stone plunks down inside my tummy. I hop away, on both feets now, to go find Sonia.

Sonia has also changed. She now can print her name and all her letters from A to Z, without the point snapping off her pencil every time. She can also count to ten like me and tie her own shoestrings. I taught her how to tie those the same way she taught me: "Sonia, try." (I found out that does work for her, after all. It just takes her a bit longer.)

She feels proud about learning all those things, but not as proud as she feels about what she's learned at recess. This is how to climb trees and drop stink bombs down on people's heads.

Actually, Alan taught Sonia to climb trees. And the stink bombs were Mitchell's idea. He always carries some of those in his pockets—gangs of slimy stink bugs, wrapped up with watered Kleenex into soggy little bags. He throws those bags from trees, mostly onto the heads of screaming girls. I never scream, though. I think stink bombs are quite interesting.

Well, one day the girl's head he threw one on was Sonia's. She did not scream either. She only stared up wobbly-eyed, stirring the bugs and Kleenex sogs around in her hairs with her fingers. But all the girls around her screamed and scattered in a million directions. I knew they would soon do worse things to Sonia than just scream. So I turned me into the lion again, headed straight for Mitchell's tree.

Lions can climb trees, even though I'm scared to by myself. When my lion digged with her pretend claws into the trunk of Mitchell's tree, he jumped down from his branch in a blur. "Hey, take it easy," he said, holding out his palms and walking backwards. "Look, I didn't do it this time to be mean to her. Okay? I'll prove it to you, kid!"

Mitchell darted up to Sonia. He carefully wiped, with an un-watered Kleenex, the bugs and the sogs from all her hairs. Then he reached into his pocket and pulled out another stink bomb. But this one he didn't throw at Sonia. Instead, he handed it to her. "You throw one at me now," he told her, smiling. "Look. I'll show you how."

And Mitchell did.

He didn't teach her how in just that recess time, of course. He tutored her for lots of recesses and Saturdays, along with Alan tutoring her how to climb trees. I tutored that sometimes too, but only when my lion jumped out and turned into me. (Other times I still feel too scaredy-cat to climb.) Sonia learned this slow, same as she learns everything. But I don't think she felt scaredy-cat like me.

Now she clings like a realife cat to the highest branch on her frontyard oak tree. The cold wind stirs that branch in circles, but Sonia in her blue coat-fur clings tight and does not fall off. "Peggy!" she calls down in her happy blurry voice. "Look at me! I Mote Thote!" That is Sonia's special name for my kitty Motorthroat.

"Be careful, Motorthroat!" I call back up to her. "And remember—kitties don't drop stink bombs down on peoples."

I should never say that, cause it makes Sonia want to do just that. And she does. Down one plops—smack on top my head with its bugs and Kleenex-sogs. "Mote Thote drops," she says, clapping and laughing. She does not laugh mean, though.

I turn me into a not-mean lion, shaking bugs and sogs from my carrot-mane. Then I claw me up that tree, plunk down next to Sonia on the next-door branch. "Lions drop, too," I tell her. "Look, there go Caitlin and Peter!"

We see them down beneath us, skipping like two my-sized kids right past our tree. They're skipping home from Peter's house, home from working on his science project without me or Alan wanted there. I remember this when Sonia hands me a stink bomb. *"Grrr!"* I roar, dropping it down hard on their heads.

But it misses, just explodes on the sidewalk behind their backs.

Maybe some things never really change.

16.

STINK BOMBS AND SNOWFLAKES

The trees are all just bones now, dancing in the wind that stirred gone all their leaves. The sky is one gray fat and furry cloud. From its mouth drop spitballs that are really flakes of snow.

"The snowflakes are Pluto people visiting Earth," I pretend today to Alan. "They're spinning down from their starships in little white parachutes."

"No, they're airplanes," Alan argues, turning into one himself. "White bombers!"

"No, Alan. Bombers kill people. That's uncool," I scold him. "You've been playing too much with that violent ol' Mitchell Brannon."

Alan airplanes round me in a circle, then dives down backwards against the freezed-hard grass. He slows his wings, pulls on his thinking face. "Actually, Pegasus, you are correct," he says at last. "About real bombers, I mean. Let's pretend these white planes carry stink bombs instead."

"Yes! Stink bombs!" I laugh and spin in circles, clapping hands. "They don't kill people, they only make them scream and plug their noses." We both plug our noses and laugh hard together. Then we turn into stink bombs ourselves, looking for some people to get screaming.

We find those people. They are Caitlin and Peter.

They're skipping home from Peter's house again, looking like two giant little kids. Caitlin's sandy hair-carrots do jumping jacks on her shoulders. Peter's glasses slip sideways off their nose-horse. Both their faces wear smiles now with sunsets sticked behind, just like the smile on Sonia when she first wrote her whole name.

"Let's get them, Alan!" I yell that in a mean voice, remembering how they wouldn't let us help them tutor Dileth. "Let's stink those smiles gone!"

So we do—but they don't. I mean their smiles don't disappear when we pounce on their bodies, Alan stinking Peter up and me stinking up old Caitlin. Instead those smiles hug us back, as huge and glowy-proud as Sonia's.

"Guess what, you guys?" That is grumpy old Caitlin, but cept she's not grumpy anymore. "We finally completed the project! It's all ready to enter in the Westlake High Science Fair."

"I hope it stinks like bugs and sogs," I tell her with a snarl. "I hope Dileth screams and plugs his nose." Actually I don't, cause my feeling mad at Caitlin isn't Dileth's fault. But Caitlin does not listen to me anyways. She only unpeels me from herself and grabs one of my stone-rolled hands. She skips me back to our house, singing what her fingers played at her last piano lesson. (Sonia's fingers can play that same song better.)

Peter listens to Alan better than Caitlin listens to me. He listens carefully to the nothing Alan says. "Hey, Einstein," he answers Alan in his old voice that is filled with quiet wind. "Something's bugging you right now. Can you tell me what it is?"

But Alan still says nothing, he only breathes out hard when he plogs into the house. Peter follows him sad-faced now, trembling and washing his soapless hands.

I grab one of those hands after letting go Caitlin's. She skips down the hall not noticing, looking for Mommy to tell about Dileth's maze. Alan races upstairs to his room. Peter starts to follow him, but his hand stays sticked in mine. "Wait, Peter," I say, before he can let go. "I can tell you what is bugging Alan."

"What is it, Pegasus?" Peter doesn't ignore me now. He steps in front of me and crouches down to just my high, his face turned into a cloud of worried-serious. I love him doing that, and I want to talk to him again.

"Alan gots a stone inside his throat when he's hurt that kills his talking. I will tell you about what made him and me feel hurt."

And I do.

Peter listens with all of him, the same way Daddy does. We plop down on the living room rug, still inside our coats and sweaters. He does not take his off or remember to unzip me. He only sits and listens, the snowflakes on his glasses melting into see-through snakes. Then more snakes slither across those glasses, these ones made from Peter's tears. "Oh wow, Pegasus," he says real soft when I'm done. "I didn't realize . . . I didn't mean to leave you guys out."

"It's okay, Peter. I forgive you, and prob'ly Alan will too. You can't help acting mean sometimes when you're round that ol' Caitlin."

"Caitlin." Peter smiles now like rainy sun. "I still can't believe she likes me, Pegasus! I feel so happy now she is actually my friend, and sometimes I forget about everyone else. But I don't want to forget you or Alan anymore. I don't want you guys to feel . . ." His face turns cloudy again. "The way I felt when Caitlin didn't like me," he goes on. "Like when she used to call me a four-eyed nerd. Do you think that's how Alan feels right now?"

"No," I tell him, smiling. "He has not four eyes, only four guinea pigs. He said animals make the *best* best friends, but 'cept for his new best friend Mitchell Brannon."

"Well, I hope he'll stick *me* on his list again, too. You guys are still my best friends—I mean besides Dileth and

Caitlin." He shyly pats my coat sleeve, then stands up fast when Mommy walks into the living room.

"Congratulations on your project, Peter." Mommy smiles up at him while she crouches down to unzip my coat. "Your parents must be so proud of your accomplishment." She and Peter talk like grown-ups about his science project. But while they talk, she also unzips his coat—just like he is sized the same as me.

That night Peter stays for supper. He spills his milk like me, and he blows his nose on his sleeve the same as Alan. But even so nobody scolds him. Caitlin does not make barfing sounds or even roll her eyes at the ceiling. She only smiles sunsets when she talks about the Science Fair.

Alan smiles sunsets too. He tells about how he also talked to Peter that afternoon, soon after I had my talk with him. "Guess what?" he asks now with dancing eyes. "Peter invited me and Pegasus to the Science Fair. We get to feed Dileth after he runs his maze!"

Caitlin nails him and Peter with her eyes, opens her mouth to argue. But Peter's eyes lock with hers and pull those nails out. Her mouth says, "Sure. Why not?" instead of arguing. Then her eyes say the same thing—and her smile is a hug around us all.

I say, "Let's turn those stink bombs back into snowflakes!"

But I think only Alan understands what I mean.

17.

FIRST PLACE WINNERS

"No, Alan. Absolutely not," Caitlin argues. "We first agreed to take you and Pegasus to the Fair, if you promised to behave like Mother said. Then she roped us into dragging along your dopey little friends. But when it comes to you taking all your old snakes and frogs and lizards and guinea pigs, I am absolutely putting my foot down."

Caitlin does, too. When she's stomping across Alan's room her foot comes down by accident smack on top of Mendel—a lizard with blue rings round him like Saturn. Her foot is bare and does not crush his back. Mendel only darts out fast across Alan's rug, his chest a puffed balloon from feeling scared. Caitlin feels scared too. She screams and jumps backwards, plopping down hard on Alan's bed. Milk swims over her face, and her eyes turn into circles like the lizard's.

"You scared each other," Alan says, observing her interested. He observes his lizard interested too, then scoops him up and sticks him back inside his box. "Don't worry, Caitlin, I won't take Mendel. He feels about humans the same way you do about lizards. But the others are lots braver, 'specially the snakes. I think the Fair will be quite educational for them."

"Spare me." Caitlin groans. "That's what Peter said about taking that Sonia kid." She frowns at me. "I know she's your friend, Pegasus, but please make sure she doesn't do anything embarrassing in front of Peter. Okay?"

"Peter wouldn't care. He likes Sonia." I sing this to Princess Leia, the garter snake looped in rings around my fingers.

"Peter likes garter snakes, too," Alan says. He pokes a mashed June bug into Princess Leia's mouth. "Taking them was actually his idea. They'll be the experiment's control, to see how untrained animals run the maze."

"Control, my foot." Caitlin grabs that foot, then rolls herself, groaning, back off Alan's bed. She stands up and flips her carrot-braids back and shakes her head at us. "You're all untrained animals, as far as I'm concerned. Who'll be *your* control?"

Me and Alan do not answer her. We only smile, observing her through the snake-rings round our fingers.

We take both snakes to the Science Fair—Princess Leia and her brother Luke. We also take Kermit the bullfrog and a guinea pig named Fang. Of course Sonia comes. Mitchell comes too. (I think he forgot about his brother Jeff saying Peter is a nerd.) And so does Haley— even though, like Mendel, she wanted to stay home.

Haley has to come with us cause of her baby sister. "Or brother," Alan reminds me. "We won't know which he'll be until he's born."

"She'll get borned any time now," I tell him. "That's why Mommy has to stay tonight with Haley's mommy. To help her push the baby out her tummy."

"Hey, Mom! Couldn't we watch?" Alan begged the night before. "When we get home from the Science Fair, can we stay at Haley's house if the baby's still not born? It would be educational for us, like the time we watched Motorthroat have her kittens."

"No!" I yelled that shivering and filled with crawly. I don't like to remember about those kittens, specially the one whose little hose got trapped around her neck—

Mommy hugged me close, chasing gone the crawly. "Pegasus is absolutely right," she said to Alan. "After the Science Fair, you are both—and Haley too—coming back home to our house and staying with Caitlin."

Alan didn't argue. He felt too excited about the Science Fair.

Peter's mommy and daddy drive us there in their big green van, cause Daddy's gone this weekend to another Writer's Conference. I hug the notebook he gave me to write notes in about the Fair. "When I show him those notes, he might turn this book into a realife science book," I say to Haley.

"So what, Margaret-pargaret? I don't care what your ol' daddy does. I'm gonna get a baby sister soon." But even so, Haley does not look happy. She frowns down at the wires on the van floor under her feets, and then she frowns at Sonia on the seat next to her. Suddenly she punches Sonia's head. "Take that, you big Dummy Head!"

Sonia roars. So does Haley—when me and Alan wave the snakes at her and Mitchell hisses. She feels scared of snakes the same way Caitlin does. Caitlin scolds us all, and Peter washes his soapless hands. Only his mommy and daddy stay calm like they didn't hear. They're talking to each other about a theory for breeding mutant fruit flies.

At the Science Fair, though, we all turn quiet. In that tall brown high school where Caitlin and Peter go, everybody else makes noise instead. The hall looks filled with people, mostly big kids sized like Caitlin and Peter and Sonia. We also see some grown-ups there and some other our-sized kids. Everybody gots machines or animals in cages. We carry them into a giant room of tables sticked with signs.

DILETH. A STUDY IN OPERANT CONDITIONING. That is what the sign in front our table says. I argue, "Dileth is not a study. He is a white rat and Peter's friend." But nobody answers me, not even Dileth. He only skitters trembling from his cage into the maze, his earthworm tail dancing to the noise.

Luke and Leia also dance, like a cageful of green pretzels. Fang both chirps and trembles, like furry brown Jell-O with a bird inside. Kermit burps like a bullfrog, which he is anyways. Haley is a scaredy-cat when it comes to animals. Now she sniffs and hiccups, but she does not roar or yell names or punch Sonia anymore.

"If you do, we'll sic the snakes on you again," I tell her in my meanest voice.

"And maybe also Dileth and Fang and Kermit the bullfrog," Alan adds.

"I'll do the bullfrog," Mitchell offers.

"I hate you, Margaret Kendall," Haley says. "And I also hate you big mean dumb ol' boys-poys! I'm telling Caitlin on you." And she does.

Caitlin likes Haley. She says that Haley's such a nice, normal little girl, that she acts the way a little sister should. "I wish you'd try to be more like her, Pegasus. And I wish you'd play with her more often, the way you used to, instead of with that weird gross-acting Sonia."

Now she crouches down and listens to Haley's whispered tattling. She listens with all of her, the same way Peter listened to me. But instead of looking mad, Caitlin's face turns all soft and sad. She pats Haley's upside-down bowl hairs. Then she stands up and takes Haley's hand and turns to Peter. "Me and Haley are going for a walk. Think you guys can manage by yourselves a little while?"

"Sure, Caitlin. Einstein here and Pegasus already know the routine, and Sonia and Mitchell will learn something new. Right, troops?" Peter grins at us when he says that, and he sounds like Daddy.

"Right!" we all answer, but cept the animals.

Dileth also knows the routine. And the others try real hard to learn something new. Luke and Leia and Fang and Kermit get all tangled up like spaghettis inside the maze, but we feed them some Dileth-leaves anyways. "They try," Sonia says, smiling and patting all their heads. "They try just like Sonia."

Lots of people swarm around to watch them try. Most of those people look sized same as Caitlin and Sonia and Peter, and they ask Peter about a million questions. The two boys who stay longest each got four eyes same as him. Their eight eyes—four of those eyes are really glasses—shine with interested while they watch Dileth run his maze. "Wow! That's really cool, man!"

Then comes Hairy Barry.

He slouches in like a crawly monster, like a cold hand squeezed around my throat. He shoves up to our table, slamming elbows into everybody else. "Flake off, you nerds!" He says that with a snarl, smiling his sharky smile. And Peter's friends flake off. I think this means go away, cause that is what they do. All but cept for me and Sonia, plus Alan and Mitchell.

Barry ignores us. He leans over the table so's his face is right up close to Peter's, aims his sharky smile just at him. "I see you got your maze here, Romeo." He talks in his most snarly voice. "Did your sweetheart pull it off your four-eyed face?"

"I—I—"

"You gonna steal any more of my women, Dr. Strangelove? You gonna try it without your trusty ol' box to protect you next time—or your sweet little white mousie?"

Peter answers nothing. He only sits there looking freezed, with milk swimming all over his face. Me and Alan and even Mitchell also freeze like statues. Only Sonia answers Barry, with Dileth in her hands. *"Grrr!"* she says, waving him in Barry's furry face.

"Hey! Keep that thing away from me!" Barry stands up straight and walks backwards with his palms facing us, just like Mitchell did that day when I first turned me into a lion. His eyes are circles same as Mitchell's too.

Dileth squeaks.

Fang chirps.

And me and Alan and Mitchell suddenly unfreeze.

"Grrr!" says Leia, poking out her tongue at Barry. (Her voice really comes from me, hiding behind her snake-rings round my fingers.)

"Grrr!" says Luke right next to her, from Alan's snake-ringed fingers. (He growls in Alan's voice.)

Kermit the bullfrog hops out Dileth's maze, puffing out his chest in a big ball. He does one long loud burp, all by himself. Then Mitchell scoops him up and makes him also say, *"Grrr!"* Same way I do when I turn into the lion.

Barry does not scream or run or flap his arms, the way Mitchell did when I roared him gone that day. But he doesn't stay either. He only snarls one of his mean old Barry-words, then he stomps away with his hands shoved into his pockets.

For just a minute, though, his eyes shoot poison arrows at us all. Their look makes the cold hand squeeze around my throat again.

Peter sags down on his chair, looking like he wants to cry. But he only looks that way a minute, cause right then Caitlin and Haley come back. And they are both bouncing, with big smiles.

"We saw a chart on how babies get made," Haley tells me, puffing out her chest like Kermit does. "I know more about that than you, Margaret-pargaret. But you are still my third-best friend."

"Guess what, Peter?" Caitlin asks. "I overheard some of the judges. And I think our project is going to win first place!"

Peter sits up straight and smiles at her like rainy sun. "That's really great," he says, sounding brave. "And things went really great here, too. Right, troops?"

"Right, Peter. 'Specially with Dileth and Fang and Luke and Leia and Kermit," Alan says. "You should be really glad we brought them, Caitlin, 'cause—"

" 'Cause they are all quite interesting." I quick interrupt him, before he can tell about Hairy Barry coming. "I think they *already* won first place."

18.

STORKS AND BABIES

"My mommy never cooks this." Haley talks in her whining skeeto voice. She glares down at the Caitlin-supper Caitlin's just dished onto her plate. This is toast with peas and tuna sticked on top, all mixed up with celery soup she poured from cans. "I hate tuna on toast. I hate it worse than liver."

"Just shut up and eat it. Okay, kid?" Caitlin says that tween her teeth, breathing a hard wind. Her eyes no longer wish for Haley to be her little sister. "You can't have everything you want in life. You're already getting a new little brother or sister, right?"

"I don't care! I want my mommy now!"

Caitlin opens her mouth to argue, but then the telephone chirps. She grabs it instead and talks in her polite-to-grown-ups voice.

"Mrs. Winthrop's invited us over to spend the evening with her," she tells us after hanging up. " 'I won't hear of four children staying alone in a house at night.' " Caitlin says that in a froggy voice, sounding like Mrs. Winthrop. "For Pete's sake, I'm fourteen," she goes on in her regular voice. "But I'll call Mom and see if I can take you kids over there. If she says yes, I can maybe go eat at Peter's house."

"I'll come to Peter's house with you, Caitlin." Haley smiles real big at her. She jumps down from her chair and grabs my sister's hand.

"You'd be bummed out, Haley," Caitlin tells her, smiling back. "I understand Peter's family always eats . . . liver!"

Haley shuts up then. She listens frowning to Caitlin's whoops when Mommy tells her yes over the phone. Then she lets my sister zip her into her coat to go see Mrs. Winthrop. "You'll like her, Haley-paley," I say, meaning Mrs. Winthrop. "She's cool! She gots lots of animals all over her tables and chairs."

"She's got birds and mammals mainly, but I like her snakes the best," Alan says. He says this in a not-mean voice, forgetting how Haley runs and screams from snakes. But Haley screams anyways. And she goes right on screaming at Mrs. Winthrop's house, even after seeing the snakes are made from not-real stuff that breaks.

"I hate meat loaf!" Haley screams that right when we walk into Mrs. Winthrop's dining room. She glares at the red lump of that sitting smack in the middle of the table, next to a plateful of those bumpy little trees.

I hate those trees, cause they're the kind called broccoli that stink like when someone used the bathroom. But I don't yell this to Mrs. Winthrop. When she spoons some onto my plate, I just wait till her back is turned. Then I sneak them quick onto Alan's plate.

Haley bursts into noisy tears. "I wanna go hoooome...."

"Oh dear, oh dear." Mrs. Winthrop trembles, washes her soapless hands. "Do hush, child. Aren't you pleased the stork is bringing your mommy a baby?"

Haley shuts up again, switching off her crying like a faucet. Her marble eyes stare hard at the bug on Mrs. Winthrop's nose. "That's dumb. Storks don't bring babies," she tells that bug. "My mommy said that's just an old wives' tale."

"Are those the same as fairy tales?" I ask Mrs. Winthrop with a smile. But she doesn't answer me, and the bug on her nose does not look happy.

STORKS AND BABIES

"Actually, Mrs. Winthrop is correct." Alan turns to Haley. "Storks do bring babies, you know. They bring baby storks."

"That's right! Let's pretend we're storks," I say through the meat loaf inside my mouth. (Sometimes a good idea makes me forget to swallow first.) "Alan can be the daddy stork, and I will be the mommy stork who's pregnant—"

"Really, children!" Mrs. Winthrop interrupts, her face colored like tomato juice. "This is hardly suitable dinner conversation, especially for little people of your tender years. Margaret, a young lady does not speak with her mouth full."

"Okay, I won't either then," I tell her after swallowing. "Can years be tender just like meat loaf or bare feets?"

Mrs. Winthrop doesn't answer me again. She excuses herself, then creaks up from her chair to plog off trembling for the dessert.

"Babies come from seeds," Haley tells us in her bossy voice, after Mrs. Winthrop's goned to the kitchen. "I know how the daddy puts the seed into the mommy."

"Everybody knows that, Haley-paley." I say this even though I don't.

"I think humans mate the same as other placental mammals," Alan says. "That would be only logical. Remember those dogs, Pegasus, the ones we saw last summer in Mrs. Green's backyard?"

"Yes." I shiver, remembering those dogs. Then I stare at Alan open-mouthed. "You mean the mommy and daddy do that too? He also stands up with his paws on her back—"

"That's dumb, Margaret-pargaret," Haley interrupts. "People don't got paws."

"—and goes inside her bottom?" I finish my question loud, to drown out Haley.

Mrs. Winthrop comes back in right when I yell that. Her trembly hands almost drop her pie, and her tomato juice face turns the color of grape juice. "Enough!" she shouts in her bullfrog voice. "We will talk about something nice." So we talk about the pie instead, which is pumpkin with whipped cream on top and even Haley's favorite. Haley eats her whole piece without screaming.

Me and Alan tell all about the Science Fair, how Dileth won first place and a fight with Hairy Barry. Haley listens quietly. Then she starts telling about the chart she saw over there, the one that explained her all about how babies get made.

This time Mrs. Winthrop interrupts. "Yes, well. It's time we cleared the table and washed these dishes, children." Her hands are trembling once again, so we all help her clear the table. And she doesn't scold me when I drop a plate made from stuff that breaks. But she doesn't answer my question either—the one about why her face keeps turning red or purple.

Suddenly her phone rings.

I jump cause it doesn't make soft bird-chirps like our phone. Instead it jangles in loud circles, like on a chainy fence when shaked by wind. It's the old-timey kind of phone, colored black instead of cream, with a circle full of holes on top instead of square-box buttons. Mrs. Winthrop also jumps, and when she tells the phone hello she jumps a second time.

"Oh, dear," she says like Jell-O after listening some more. "Do you really think it's wise to have them over there so soon? I hardly would consider it suitable, you know. In my day . . ."

She stops and listens more, so I never get to hear the new story about her day. (Mrs. Winthrop's day happened a long-long time ago. It must have been a super-long day, cause so many different things happened to her on it. All of them are very interesting.) Her face soon turns tomato juice, then grape again. This looks almost as interesting as the stories she tells about her day.

"Very well," she says at last and hangs up. When she turns to speak to us, her lips look like two needles sewing shut her mouth. Puckers like pulled cloth show on her skin around those needles. "Well, I never." She poofs out hard wind. "Children. Alan, Margaret. You too, Little Girl," she says to Haley, whose realife name she never can remember. "Fetch your coats and put them on and zip them up, my dears. I must take you all at once over to your house, Little Girl—"

"My name is Haley, an' I'm not a little girl! Mommy says I'll soon be the big sister!"

"Yes, well, child. You mustn't interrupt. Your mother has a very nice surprise for you, you see. Wouldn't you like to go on home and see what it is?"

"Tell me, tell me first! Is it the newest baby Cabbage Patch doll?"

"Why, no. It's actually . . . well, a lovely surprise brought by the stork."

"A baby stork?" Alan guesses, looking hopeful. That is the exact wrong thing to say, cause it gets Haley screaming again like a red siren.

"Gross!" She twists away when Mrs. Winthrop tries to zip her coat. "I don't wanna yucky ol' bird-brained baby stork! I want the newest baby Cabbage Patch doll. . . ."

"Well, you're not getting anything if you behave like this. I've never seen such dreadful manners." Mrs. Winthrop's face puffs up big when she scolds Haley. Even the brown bug on her nose puffs up big. She frowns at us more bullfroggy than I've seen her do since the time she was not yet our friend.

"I wanna go *hooooome!*" Haley sobs harder. She charges to the front door with her coat hanging half off, till me and Alan each grab her by an empty sleeve. We catch a blue coat filled with only air instead of Haley. Mrs. Winthrop's door bangs shut, with Haley screaming bare-armed on the wrong outside of it.

"Oops!" me and Alan say together.

"Oh dear, oh dear." Mrs. Winthrop is washing her soapless hands again. We all look at each other. Then we all rush pushing out the door in one fat clump.

I find Haley scrunched up tight into a ball, right between Mrs. Winthrop's house-boards and her bell-shaped bushes dressed in sparkly snow. She's shaking so cold her tears have turned into ice-snakes on her cheeks. "Listen, Haley-paley," I say, stuffing empty coat sleeves with her goosebumped arms. "I think I know what is your surprise. It's not a baby stork, but a baby human being. Just like you and your mommy."

"Well, 'course I know that, you silly Margaret-pargaret." Haley snuffles. "You think I'm a baby too? But it's still not fair, 'cause that baby is Mommy's surprise and not for me. I want *my* surprise to be the newest baby Cabbage Patch doll." And Haley sobs and screams some more, though this time she does it still enough for me to zip her coat.

Sometimes, only sometimes, I think Haley is a pain. Specially in my ears, like balloons popping.

We plog across the squishy snow, past my house to Haley's next door. My mommy answers Haley's door instead of Haley's mommy. Haley ducks beneath her arm and gallops to the sofa, which like always is heaped with yarny blankets. Haley's mommy knits these and sells them at the boutique store downtown. They are made from strings, with many holes that let the light peek through like diamonds.

Only now the holes got pink skin peeking through them stead of light. Most of this pink skin belongs to Haley's mommy, cause she's curled up like a cat beneath the blanket. But some of it belongs to the tiny baby curled right next to her.

"Hi, Haley's sister!" I greet the tiny baby with a wave.

"Brother," corrects Haley's smiling string-haired mommy. She turns her sagging smile onto Haley. "Meet your brother Justin Ryan, honey."

I stiff myself for siren-screams, cause Haley's always told me her baby is a sister. But Haley's body stays a statue and her mouth a quiet cave. Then the blanket lifts up for her to dive beneath. Its light-holes become pink again, filled with Haley too.

"Won't she give the baby germs?" Mrs. Winthrop's fish eyes swim with worried. But Mommy only laughs right along with Haley's mommy, and she pulls us all in closer for a peek. "Oh, he's just adorable!" Mrs. Winthrop cries. A smile curls up on her cheeks that makes her eye-fish sparkle.

"His nose looks slightly like a beak," Alan observes with interested. "Maybe he's a hybrid, half human and half stork, and the daddy stork is the one who brought him. Do you think that might be possible, Haley?"

"Don't be so dumb, you big ol' boy-poy! Don't you even know where babies come from? I learned all about it from the chart at Peter's Science Fair. See, the daddy puts his sperm—"

Haley's mommy clamps a hand tight over Haley's mouth. She starts talking many words like snowflakes to my mommy, and Mommy talks right back with even more words. The words dance fast like snowflakes twirling in a wind, then break up into bubbles of pink laughing.

Everyone is laughing now—everybody but cept the baby and Mrs. Winthrop. He just stays sleeping, and she begins sewing more face-cloth with her needle-lips. Both their faces are the color of tomato juice.

19.

ALONE

Justin Ryan's face looks just a teensy bit like Mrs. Winthrop's. It's round and slightly wrinkled, with egg hair sticked on top. But cept instead of scrambled eggs, Justin's hair is raw egg smeared across his head in cloudy strings. His nose is the same size as the bug on Mrs. Winthrop's nose, only red instead of brown. His whole face looks red usually, same as Mrs. Winthrop's gets whenever we talk about where babies come from.

Mommy says her face-red is because of a feeling called *embarrassed.* That means not wanting to hear about private things, like bare bottoms or going to the bathroom. It also means how Mommy feels when I talk about those things round Mrs. Winthrop.

"But what makes Justin Ryan's face turn red?" I ask Mommy that this morning, after we get home from Haley's house.

It is now Christmas vacation, and I go there every morning with Mommy. She helps Haley's mommy with the baby, while I argue with Haley about a scary pretend man named Sandy Claws.

"I don't think he feels embarrassed," I tell Mommy now, meaning that baby Justin Ryan. "He smiles when you wash his bare bottom in the sink and when he uses his diaper for a bathroom."

"I don't really know what makes him turn red, Pegasus. Newborns simply come that color sometimes. You were born red, and so was Alan."

"What color was Caitlin? Off-beige with a touch of mauve?" Those are Caitlin's favorite colors. I'm not sure how they look, but she's always begging Mommy to let her paint her room with them.

Mommy laughs and nods. "Actually she was, though I never would have thought to describe her colors that way. She was off-beige when sleeping, and mauve while awake and screaming bloody murder."

"Justin Ryan doesn't scream 'bloody murder.' He just screams *'aaaaaaa,'* like a siren with a million grains of sand spraying through it. When he screams that, his red face mixes up with purple. Is that color mauve? Can you turn mauve even if you don't scream 'bloody murder'? Even if you scream *'aaaaaaa'* instead? Why do you think Justin Ryan turns that color anyways? Do you think maybe it's 'cause—"

"Aaaaaaaaaaa!" Mommy screams. She turns mauve herself (I think) and plugs her ears. Then she frowns at me and tells me to stop asking her questions.

"Who can I ask them then, Mommy?"

"Go find your brother, he'll give you answers." She breathes slow wind, all sagging-tired. "Between your endless questions, and Alan's endless lectures about fruit fly reproduction, and Haley's endless bragging that she knows more than he does about human reproduction, and her mother always worrying about what she knows, and Mrs. Winthrop scolding us both every day about the shocking things we teach our children . . . Well, you're all about to drive me crazy!"

"I don't think I will, 'cause I don't know how to drive yet. Where is Crazy?"

This time she says nothing, but she looks the way she does when she tells us one more word will make her blow her stack. So off I skip to find my brother Alan. Maybe, only maybe, he'll answer my questions instead.

But he doesn't.

"Pegasus, I'm busy now." That is all old Alan says to me. He and Mitchell Brannon are plopped down on the rug next to his bed, staring at the fruit flies inside Alan's bug box. He's been breeding them since last summer, warm under lights inside his room. He and Mitchell hope the flies will have mutant four-winged babies, the same kind Peter's mommy and daddy talk about.

"Quit bugging me, okay?" Alan says that when I peek inside the box, even though I joggle him just by accident. He grins then and giggles, but cept not at me. He's laughing at these lace-winged flies zipping out the box, landing and taking off some jam streaks on his arms. "I don't mean you guys, though," he tells the flies. Then he turns his silly grin up to that old Mitchell. "I only want bugs to bug me. Get it?"

"Hey yeah, that's cool! We only want bugs to bug us, man—not little sisters!"

I stomp out mad from Alan's room, which is now filled with boy-poy howling laughs. That old Mitchell's turned mean again, just like he used to be. But cept now he turns his mean on only me, not Alan too. And sometimes he pulls Alan into his mean right along with him.

When he does this, I feel very much Alone.

I've been feeling Alone that way a whole lot too much lately. Everyone's been gone this week I can ever play with—all but cept for that pain of a Haley-paley, who only wants to whine about her baby brother and argue with me about old Sandy Claws.

My friends Ashley and Danielle are both gone with their families to visit Grandma and Grandpa. (I mean theirs, not ours, cause we already went to visit ours for Thanksgiving dinner. Daddy said if we drove those miles to visit them again, we'd have to eat tuna stead of turkey for Christmas dinner.) Even Sonia's gone, practicing piano for our church's Christmas pageant. She'll play the music for that on Christmas Eve.

Caitlin, of course, still spends all her time with Peter. Plus she gots a girl best friend, a new one named Rachel who reads fat books with her. They got stories about science things, pretend ones that didn't happen yet but might someday. Caitlin won't let me read those books. She says they're too scary for little kids. And when I argue, she still calls me Pegasus the Pest.

Daddy's gone to another Writer's Conference. More people like his books than they did last year, and they keep on asking him to go explain them how he wrote his stories. He won't be home till the night before Christmas Eve.

Mommy yells at him sometimes cause she thinks he's gone too much—specially with Christmas coming soon. She also yells at us more cause she's so busy with Christmas. She says it will Drive Her Crazy if we don't do that first. I didn't know Christmas could drive either. And I don't understand why it's making her turn stripy-red and yelling.

Usually, Christmas is my favorite holiday. It's a green and furry tree spicing up the living room and chewy cookie-stars spicing up the kitchen. It is popcorn beads and silver bells and red balls you can see your face inside unless they break. (Motorthroat always breaks at least three.) It is rainbow fairy-lights and dancing songs about a donkey, sheep and kings and camels and a Baby sleeping on top a crib filled up with hay.

The Baby is my very most favorite part of all.

He's not screaming-red like Justin Ryan. He's always sleeping with a secret smile on His face, a glowy rainbow smile like the one His mommy wears when she peeks out from inside her long blue bathrobe. That smile makes the fairy lights go dancing all through me. And the secret smile comes on my face too.

I know the Baby's secret. Daddy told me. It's that He's really God, but a realife baby newly borned right at the same time. I don't know much about God, but cept He made us all and He lives beyond the clouds. I also think He likes to eat lettuce, cause in Sunday School we say this verse: *I was glad when they said unto me, "Lettuce, go into the house of the Lord."* I can't see Him, though, so I can't ask Him what He does with all that lettuce.

The Baby I can see, and I think He is too little to eat lettuce. He probly just drinks milk straight from His mommy, like Justin Ryan does. I can understand God better as a Baby. But cept He doesn't talk, and His skin feels hard and woody instead of silky-warm like Justin Ryan's. So today I set Him back down in His crib beneath the tree. I want to talk to someone who will talk back to me, and who will swallow gone all my Alone. I also want to hold a realife baby with silk skin.

So off I trot back over to Haley-paley's house. I sneak out my house fast, without stopping to pull my coat down from the closet. I just hurry bare-armed through the snow and icy wind. This is cause I don't want Mommy to catch me going and say *Don't bother them.*

I need them all right now. I need baby Justin Ryan and his mommy all sleepy-pink beneath their blanket, and even bossy old Haley with her talk about Sandy Claws And I specially need Mrs. Winthrop, who answers *this* next door now cause she helps in the afternoons with Justin Ryan.(She takes turns afternoons with Mr. Emmett, who helps with Justin Ryan whenever he's not giving piano lessons.) *She* never says *Go find Alan* or *Don't bug me.*

"Come in, child, before you catch your death of cold!" That is what she always says, and she cries that extra loud today. "Whatever can your mother be thinking, letting you go outside dressed like that?"

"She's thinking 'bout both us and Christmas driving her crazy. May I please have a cup of hot chocolate with whipped cream?"

"Why certainly, child. You need something hot to warm you up. These young mothers these days!" She scolds as she plogs to the stove. But she smiles when she set the yellow Big Bird mug in front me, the one filled with brown and white and steam and cream-sweet hotness. The hotness burns my tongue, but then it melts warm my freezed insides.

"Where is Justin Ryan?" I ask when I have drinked it gone.

"The poor little dear is with his mother now . . . ah, having his lunch. In *my* day we used a bottle." She sniffs. "And we'd never dream of exposing a baby at so young an age to the public. Acting in a Christmas pageant, of all things!" Mrs. Winthrop sounds scolding again, though not at me. "I tell her she'll regret it if that child takes a cold. But do these young people ever listen?"

"They do sometimes," I answer her, thinking about all the young people I know. "When they're not reading scary science books about the future or feeding jam to mutant fruit flies or laughing with their mean ol' friends or arguing about Sandy Claws—"

"Oh, please do hush, Margaret. I've a million things to do." She sounds scolding at *me* now. "Go find young Haley. Maybe you can persuade her to stop sulking in her room."

Haley isn't sulking. She's lying on her rug writing a letter. But cept Haley writes her letters with only lots of dots and lines and squiggles. When I open her bedroom door, she screams and crushes her paper into a crinkly snowball. Then she throws it down to join the other

ALONE

snowballs sprinkled all around her. "I hate you!" she yells, but at the snowballs not at me.

"Why do you hate those snowballs?" I ask her from the door.

"Don't be dumb, Margaret-pargaret. Those aren't snowballs, they are just crumpled-up ol' papers. I hate those dumb ol' papers! They won't make my words right when I write to Sandy Claws."

Sandy Claws is also dumb, I want to argue with her. He's a scary booming giant who plops himself in all the stores right before Christmas. He's all tomato-red, but cept for a snowy beard that pokes out from his chin and scratches people. Mommy and Daddy say he's just pretend. But he scares me anyways, cause I think he might be made from sand and have claws on his wrists instead of hands. Haley says that's dumb and that anyways, he's real. We argue about him all the time.

Only now I do not argue, cause Haley looks too sad. She's crying like the time I first drew peoples from other planets. I run wrap my arms round her and let her tears rain down and wet my shirt. "It's okay, Haley-paley."

"No, it's not!" Haley twists out from my arms. "If Sandy Claws can't read my letter, how will he know to bring me my new baby Cabbage Patch doll?"

"I'll write the letter for you, Haley-paley." But a new idea jumps inside me when I pick up Haley's pencil. "I know! Why don't you write to Baby Jesus 'stead of Sandy Claws? He's too little to read, so He won't care if your words come out in those crookedy squiggles. I bet He can read those squiggles, 'cause He is also God. Even though He's just a tiny Baby."

"I hate that Baby!" Haley yells. She grabs her pencil back from me and throws it across her room. "It's not fair, Justin Ryan gets to be Him in the Christmas pageant. I don't get to be Him, I don't get to be nothing at all! Even though I'm bigger. I wish Mommy would throw away that dumb ol' baby brother." Haley's crying hard again. She's rolled up in a ball just like her papers turned to snowballs, but cept bigger and wearing clothes and colored pink instead of white.

I feel ice growing inside me. It freezes the sweet hot chocolate to a cold and sour lump inside my tummy. How can Haley hate a Baby who is also God? And how can she want her mommy to throw away her baby brother? "Don't say all those mean things, Haley-paley," I scold her. Then I try to hug her tears and hurting gone again.

"Stop it! Leave me alone!" Haley jerks out from my arms and turns, punches my tummy. "Go away, you dumb ol' Margaret-*pargaret!* I hate you too!"

Those words hit me harder than her fist against my tummy.

I plog back to the living room, looking for someone to comfort me. But nobody gots comfort, only angry.

The angry is red siren-screams that come from Justin Ryan, who keeps pounding and kicking Mrs. Winthrop.

It is grumble-glares on Mrs. Winthrop's tired face, while she stomps around jiggling her arms filled up with baby.

And, worst of all, it is the yelling from my mommy.

She's come scolding through the snow over here to Haley's house. She shakes me and spanks me right in front of Mrs. Winthrop, then she stuffs me hard inside two sweaters and my fattest hoody coat. "How dare you run off like this without telling me? Without even bothering to put your coat on in this freezing weather, worrying me half to death?"

But I am crying too hard now to answer her question. Alone has pounced and swallowed me up completely gone.

20.

TWO BABIES AND A MAN

It's Christmas Eve, and still I don't feel sparkly.

I bet tonight at the Christmas pageant, Haley will still not talk to me. A whole week has passed since that day she punched my tummy, and she's still filled up with angry. Not only at me, but also at her mommy and her brother Justin Ryan. And tonight I think she feels more angry than she ever did before. Because tonight at our church is when Justin Ryan gets to turn into Baby Jesus.

Of course I know he doesn't really. The realife Jesus is not even a Baby anymore. He's a grown-up Man who died and came alive again and went to Heaven. I don't like to think about that Man, cause He scares me almost bad as Sandy Claws.

In the picture on the yellow wall in my Sunday School class, He looks a little bit like Sandy Claws. He's holding a my-sized little girl on His lap, just like Sandy Claws does with the my-sized children at the stores. How can that girl be so brave? I always wonder. Same way I wonder that about those kids who sit on Sandy Claws.

In some ways, though, the Man in the picture looks not so scary. He's skinny and quiet stead of big and booming, and He wears a soft white bathrobe stead of red clothes that roar loud like *ho-ho-ho's.* Also, His beard looks brown instead of white like frozen snow. Still, it's big enough to touch and scratch the little girl on His lap. Plus, the mouth beneath that beard is never smiling. It looks straight and skinny, like a needle.

But what always scares me most about that picture is His eyes. They look all black and burny, like the holes in Alan's blanket that came when Mommy left the iron on too long. I feel scared those eyes could burn straight through me. They could see all the bad in me that made the Man have to die the way He did. . . . And that's the part about Him that scares me worst of all.

Specially tonight.

You see, tonight I am still filled with angry, same as Haley. Even though tonight is Christmas Eve. I still feel mad at the whole world! I hate not just Haley and her screaming baby brother, but also cranky Mrs. Winthrop and spanking-scolding Mommy and bossy old Caitlin and even Alan, who's turned all this week as mean as Mitchell. I even hate Daddy, cause he's just stayed sleeping since he got home yesterday from his Writer's Conference. Mommy only now pulled him out of bed to get dressed for the pageant.

"Don't wanna go to that dumb ol' Christmas pageant!" I stomp and scream, the same as Haley.

Whatever's gotten into you, Pegasus? That's what I *wish* Mommy would ask me. Even if she shaked me then and poofed a tired wind, she would still be paying me attention.

Angry's gotten into me, I could explain to her. *Not like those other years at Christmas, when dancing lights and cookies got into me.* And then I'd tell her why, and I'd turn her shaking hands into hugging ones.

But Mommy *doesn't* ask me that. She only just tells me, "I'm fed up with you, young lady." She says that tween her teeth, like Alan's hissing snakes. Then she storms out to the hall and yells, "Hurry up!" to Daddy and Alan and Caitlin.

I feel Ignored again.

I feel swallowed by Alone.

At church I am bologna stuffed tween people like a sandwich. Daddy makes up one bread and Mrs. Winthrop the other bread. The inside layers of bologna are made from Mommy and me and Haley and Caitlin and Alan and Mrs. Gray, who is Sonia's mommy. (Not Sonia, of course, cause she is sitting way up front behind the big piano, playing "Away in a Manger.") But sometimes you can feel Alone even being bologna in the middle.

I still feel Alone, even here in church. I guess Haley next to me feels even more Alone, cause her mommy and daddy don't sit with her on the bench like mine do. Her daddy ran away last April with another lady, and he's miles gone this Christmas. And her mommy, though she is right here inside the church, doesn't sit this year with Haley.

Instead, she's sitting way up front facing all the people, smiling at them from inside her long blue bathrobe. Her tonight-name, just pretend, is Mary. And Joseph sitting next to her is really my piano teacher Mr. Emmett.

I know both these things fill Haley up with angry. But most of her angry comes not from her mommy or Mr. Emmett, or even from her daddy who ran away. Most comes from her baby brother Justin Ryan, who lays curled up in her mommy's arms pretending to be Baby Jesus.

"I hate him!" she yells now, right out loud in church.

Several people turn and whisper, *"Shhhh!"* Mrs. Winthrop looks what Caitlin calls *mortified.* Mommy and Daddy look worried, and Alan and Caitlin just ignore her. Only for a second, I feel sad for Haley swim through me instead of angry. And I'm the only one who tries to comfort her.

"It's not fair, is it?" I whisper, petting her Jell-O-shaking back. "You should get to sit up front with your mommy and your brother. But don't worry, Haley-paley, you didn't get left out 'cause they don't love you. You just got left out 'cause Baby Jesus didn't have a big sister."

"I hate Him!" Haley yells again, even louder this time. "And I hate you too, you dumb ol' Margaret-*pargaret!*"

And then she punches me.

Again.

Really hard.

Right in the same place she did last week. Smack in the middle of my tummy.

I don't punch her back. And nobody else spanks or even scolds her. But now they don't ignore her anymore. She's just burst into tears, so they all swarm around her like a cloud of bees round flowers. But cept they're humming with soft whispers stead of buzzing, and they're touching her with fingers stead of stingers.

Then hugging her.

Cradling her.

Whispering comfort-words like drops of honey.

But they all keep on ignoring me.

And it's just too much.

"I HATE YOU!"

I yell that at Everyone. Everyone in the church and the whole world.

Well, almost.

There is one Person I feel quite sure will comfort me.

I break free from Everyone Else, skooch tween all those layers in the sandwich to the outside of it. Then I run and run and run, down and down the doggie-tongue that's actually the long red rug leading to up front.

I push through shepherds and Wise Men that turn into grunting boys. Squeeze past angel wings that bend into cardboards glued with cotton balls like bunny tails. I do not say I'm sorry to the mostly my-sized angels sticked between them. Instead, I just fly straight toward the mommy—the kitty-voiced, string-haired mommy in the long blue bathrobe who sometimes, only sometimes, I wish could be my mommy stead of Haley's.

Only tonight she's turned into the mommy of Baby Jesus—and He's the One I actually came to see. The Baby will comfort me, cause He is God and understands everything. Even about feeling Alone and things being Unfair—

Whomp! I smack hard against a mommy-tummy that is no longer filled with baby. The tummy's body jerks backwards, and the baby in its arms wakes up.

And screams!

He's no longer Baby Jesus, soft and pink and smiling secret knowing inside His dreams. He's turned into Justin Ryan, all purple and red and screaming like a siren. Or like his big sister, mean old Haley.

I scream along with him. Then I turn again and race right off that stage. I head, not down the red tongue that would slurp me back inside that people sandwich, but instead through a secret black door.

The hall outside looks also black, but I run down it anyways. Running through even black feels better than getting punched or spanked inside red and green and silver. And Alone down a long hall feels better than Alone stuffed inside a giant people sandwich.

But cept I am no longer Alone.

The crying comes from one of the doors on my right side. (I know it is my right side cause Alan drew a star on top my hand to show that side, plus a moon on top my other hand to show my wrong side.) The crying sounds silver-sad, not angry like a red and bleeding siren. I follow it through the black till it turns loud behind a door. Then I open that door to find out who is making it.

Haley-paley.

I know this cause I see her, clear in the bright room turned yellow from the light switch clicked to "up" on the wall. The bright room is our Sunday School, all cheerful with books and rugs and toys and tea sets and piano. Everything is there but cept our teacher Mrs. Davies and the Sunday swarm of pushing, wiggling my-sized other children. Even all the Bible pictures on the walls are there.

All of them but cept for one.

In the empty space like in Alan's mouth where his two front teeth fell out last year, there is usually sticked that scary picture of the brave little girl sitting on Jesus' lap. Not Baby Jesus, but Scary Grown-up Man Jesus with His beard and burny eyes. Only now instead of on the wall, that picture is peeking up from Haley's hands.

She sits curled against the wall below its empty space, smiling down at the picture in her hands like rainy sun. She is no longer crying. Tears have turned into stiff and see-through snakes all down her cheeks, but her mouth moves not with sob-sounds but with words. "Daddy," she is saying over and over to the picture. "I love you, Daddy...."

That's not your daddy, I almost tell her.

But Someone stops me.

I cannot see Someone, but I can feel Him. He doesn't stop me with yells or scolding words or spanking hands. Instead, He takes one of my own hands (the right one with the star) and leads me over to sit down next to Haley-paley. I feel Him there like love inside my tummy stead of hate, like grassy warm instead of icy stone.

I no longer hate Haley.

And she no longer hates me either.

Instead she hands me the picture and we look at it, sharing it together. The eyes of the Man in it look sparkly now instead of burny. And His mouth is not a needle, but a smile.

Me and Haley smile back, turning into two little girls who sit together on His lap. And we don't even push or punch to force each other off. There is room for both of us together—

"There they are!"

Everybody Else yells that out at the same time. And into the warm and grassy room they all explode: Daddy and Alan and Caitlin and Mrs. Winthrop and Mrs. Gray and Sonia and Mr. Emmett and Haley's mommy and my mommy too. But nobody this time spanks or yells or scolds—not even Mommy. Me and Haley hug each other. Then we both get snatched and lifted high and locked tight into hugs from all the grown-ups. And we both end up inside our mommies' arms.

Then outside on the church front grass, Daddy takes a camera picture. It shows the First Christmas once again, with Mary and Joseph and Baby Jesus. But this time there are two new people in the family—two big sisters named Haley and Pegasus.

And now Mary is really Haley's mommy, and Joseph is only my piano teacher Mr. Emmett. But Justin Ryan, once again asleep in his mommy's arms, had turned back into Baby Jesus. When I touch one pointer finger to His pink and silky cheek, His lips curve up into a secret smile. It's a warm and grassy smile that is full of love and knowing—the same one I just saw on the picture of the Man.

And He chases gone all my Alone.

21.

WASHING KITTY CLEAN

Christmas Day starts out all sparkly.

Me and Alan sneak downstairs like we always do, inching through the part of morning colored midnight-black. That's the first part of morning, so Mommy and Daddy and Caitlin are still sleeping.

We sneak into the living room and shake our presents neath the spicy tree. "It's a hard rectangle that doesn't rattle," I observe about the first one, whispering to Alan. "I think it might be a book, the new one Daddy wrote for me."

"I wish Daddy could build for me a new computer," Alan whispers back like a sad wind. "This package feels soft and slightly shapeless. I unfortunately think it's only socks."

"Your computer's made from socks?"

"Of course not, Dummy. I meant this present." He sets it down and thinks a minute. "You're not being logical, Pegasus. Socks have no electronic capabilities. How could they operate a disk drive?"

"Very softly," I answer him, speaking softly too. "So softly you couldn't hear their buttons clicking."

Alan groans and slaps his forehead, the way he learned how to do from Mitchell Brannon. He learned to call me Dummy from Mitchell Brannon too. Before they became friends he always called me only Pegasus. But this morning I feel too sparkly inside to mind. Besides, Alan's groaning turns into giggling. I catch the giggle-bug from him, and soon we both wake everybody up.

"Children!" Caitlin also groans as she plogs into the room, braiding her long hairs into soft and sandy carrots.

But she isn't really mad. Nobody is really mad on Christmas Morning. Our inside-smiles soon peek out to match the smile on the Baby.

This morning I smile right back at that Baby. I share His secret, about Him really being the Man who smiled at me last night from His picture in the Sunday School room. I wonder if the Man, not Sandy Claws, brought me some presents.

We won't find out till afternoon. That's when we open presents, after our turkey dinner with Everybody Here.

Everybody Here changes every year. Last year it was Grandma and Grandpa, but this year we ate Thanksgiving turkey with them instead at their house. This Christmas they have gone to a state called Florida. So Everybody Here will be Haley and her mommy and her brother Justin Ryan. Plus Mr. Emmett, who is coming with them too—cause he's turned into the very best friend of Haley's mommy. And also Mrs. Winthrop, who's a good friend to us all.

And, best of all, my friend Sonia.

Mr. Emmett's excited about Sonia coming too, cause he wants to hear her play more Christmas songs on our piano. "She's truly phenomenal," he told us again last night after the Christmas pageant. "She's perhaps the most brilliant student I've ever had."

"It's not fair." Caitlin's whining now like a creaky door. "Why can't Peter come too? He's truly phenomenal at running experiments—the most brilliant scientist I've ever known."

"And why can't Mitchell come?" Alan argues too. "He's truly phenomenal at dropping stink bombs, Mom."

"That's what I'm afraid of," Mommy tells him, shaking her head. "Now listen, you two, this whining has got to stop. 'Tis the season to be jolly. . . . Besides, remember that both Peter and Mitchell have their grandparents visiting this Christmas. Poor Sonia, on the other hand, has nobody but us. Her mother's down with the flu today, I'm afraid."

Nobody else feels afraid, only grumping. All but cept for me. I still feel sparkly enough to dance Motorthroat round the tree. While we dance, I sing. "I got *two* friends coming today, both Sonia and Haley-paley...."

"Mo-om! Make her shut up!" Caitlin and Alan yell that at the same time.

"That's enough, everyone." That is Mommy, in her voice like a spanking hand. "Can it, Margaret Kendall!"

"Mrrrooowwww!" That is Motorthroat. Even she is grumping now, cause I just tied a ribbon to her tail striped red-and-green for Christmas.

I can it. This means not that I put something in a can like vegetables, but that I stop singing and dancing Motorthroat. Plus, I pull the ribbon off her tail soon's she spanks my nose. But I still feel sparkly inside, even though her spanking left two stinging red train tracks down my nose. (I can tell cause I see them in the long hallway mirror.)

Next to my nose, Motorthroat at Christmas likes spanking ornaments. She now slaps one off the tree and chases it across the rug. It is a snowball made from drinking cup stuff that doesn't break, so nobody takes this one from her. But she bounces it into the pot where lives the dirt that feeds our tree, and some dirt bounces out onto the rug.

Mommy groans again, cause just then the doorbell dings.

Behind the door stands Haley. She's clutching the left hand of her mommy, whose baby Justin Ryan now hangs outside her tummy inside a strappy bag. On their other side stands Mr. Emmett, who's clutching the *right* hand of Haley's mommy. Mrs. Winthrop stands next to him. And tween them both, holding on tight to both their hands, stands my best friend Sonia.

In they all troop with snow-puddles leaking behind their boots, right when Daddy still is sweeping dirt into the tree pot. Off come all their boots and coats and scarves, while Mommy sparkle-talks to them. Away slink Caitlin and Alan, still grumping a little about no Peter or Mitchell being here. And up springs Motorthroat, no longer grumping now but playing. She chases another ornament—straight up top the tree.

This one falls and breaks. Daddy stays real busy with his broom. Motorthroat gets spanked with it off into the bathroom, where she starts grumping once again.

"Oh dear, oh dear." That is Mrs. Winthrop, washing her hands without soap. Mr. Emmett starts doing that and saying it too, but Haley's mommy laughs so instead he laughs right with her. And instead of washing his soapless hands he keeps his right hand tucked around her left hand, then he tries to wrap his other hand round Haley's. But Haley twists away from him, looking *really* grumping. And Sonia just looks like an empty paper.

Even so, I still feel sparkly inside. "Hi, Sonia! Hi, Haley-paley!" I shout that like silver bells, smiling and taking both their hands. "Merry Christmas, both my friends!"

Haley's face scrinches up into a wrinkly prune. *"I'm your friend. Just me, not that Dummy Head,"* she argues. "Plus, that ol'Emmett man is *not* my daddy."

"He my piano teacher," Sonia says. "And I Sonia, Peggy's friend. Not Dummy Head."

"You're Sonia Head," I tell her with a smile. "And Haley is Haley Head, and I'm a horse with wings. And we are all three of us best friends with each other." *I hope,* I think inside myself. Out loud I say, "On Christmas. 'Cause that is the rule at our house."

Haley looks like she might scream, *I wanna go hoooome!* But fortunately, as Alan would say, Motorthroat explodes out the bathroom once again. This time she catches *two* ornaments, and Everybody chases her. All but cept for me and Sonia and even Haley, cause we all laugh and clap together at my kitty's show.

At dinner Everybody laughs, even all the grown-ups. And even Haley-paley likes the food. Turkey legs taste better than meat loaf or toast with tuna, so she chews and swallows and smiles stead of whining. She even smiles once at her brother Justin Ryan, who smiles right back at her stead of screaming.

Only he eats not turkey or cranberries or pumpkin pie, but milk straight from beneath his mommy's blouse. Mrs. Winthrop looks everywhere else but cept at that, her face swimming with tomato juice. But this time she doesn't talk about how babies drank from bottles in her day. She just tells Mommy—mine this time—how lovely she's prepared everything.

After dinner, Everybody Here keeps on acting sparkly. It's time to open presents neath the tree. The grown-ups take forever peeling little curlies from their boxes, stopping first forever to read their fancy cards. The kids all tear the paper off their boxes in one second, tossing it plus cards and ribbons across the room for Motorthroat to chase. Those things are *her* presents, and they keep her from chasing ornaments.

The grown-ups get things like soaps and ties and scarves, bottles of stinky stuff that make them smile anyways. They act all excited, even though that stuff looks really boring. Caitlin gets all clothes, which me and Alan also think is boring. (Actually, I think it's *board*ing, which means even worse than boring.) But she acts all happy about them, same as the grown-ups.

Alan's first favorite present is a new computer, even though he also gets some socks. And mine is Daddy's book—he one he wrote just for me—though that's the present I pick out last.

Sonia also gets a book, a skinny one with pictures she can read all by herself. This present is her favorite too. She reads it to us over and over, till Haley tells her it is just a baby book. But when Haley gets her Cabbage Patch doll, the one surprise she wanted, she's so happy she lets Sonia feed her present with its bottle.

"Sandy Claws brought her," she tells me, like she won a game.

"No, he didn't. Baby Jesus did." I argue like the game is not yet over.

"Whoa, there!" Daddy says, raising one hand. "How about this, young scamps? Maybe Baby Jesus told Sandy Claws to bring her. Maybe the old guy works for Baby Jesus."

"Really, James!" Mommy shakes her head at him, clicking her tongue.

But Alan grins and says, "That sounds logical, Dad." And the more I think about it, the more it really does. Maybe Sandy Claws gots people hands and skin like everybody else. Maybe God made him the same way He made me. Anyways, Daddy's words stop the game tween me and Haley. We decide we both won it and quit. And we both turn sparkly once again.

Then comes Alan's second favorite present.

Sonia brought it. The box looks miles bigger than the one she brought for me, the one holding three empty books for writing stories in. I feel, for one second, what Mommy would call *jealous*. But when Alan tears it open I instead felt sorry for him, cause that box looks like it gots just dirt inside.

"Hey, cool!" Alan grins at the dirt, his eyes shining like he's seeing golden fairy dust. At first I think he is only being nice to Sonia, till I see the tunnels snaking through that dirt. Because inside all those tunnels race these funny-looking small black bugs.

Each bug is made from three balls, all sticked together in one body. From every ball sprout two legs. And every bug, like all insects, gots six of those legs.

"An ant farm!" Alan laughs and claps, and he even wraps up Sonia in a hug.

"Does the farm got tiny cows?" I ask, but Alan only laughs a second time. I look for myself. It doesn't. No cows or chickens or pigs or horses live inside those tunnels, only ants running on all six legs.

But all at once, that changes.

All at once that ant farm gots not only ants inside, but also the paw of a giant kitty—

"Motorthroat!" We all yell that, Everybody Here. Alan grabs for her, but she kicks over his farm. Miles of dirt bounce out onto the rug. It's more than the tree pot's dirt, plus with ants inside. And nobody looks sparkly anymore.

Mrs. Winthrop screams. So do Mommy and Caitlin and Haley. Mr. Emmett says, "Oh, dear!" He washes his soapless hands this time, and Haley's mommy tries to comfort him. Daddy runs to grab the broom again.

Alan starts picking up the ants. Some of those ants bite him, and he starts screaming too. His arms flap up and knock against the coffee table, where sits Mrs. Winthrop's cup of after-dinner coffee.

The coffee cup flips over and pours coffee on the dirt.

The dirt turns into coffee-stinking mud.

Motorthroat likes to roll in mud. Even when it stinks like coffee.

And she does.

Until Sonia catches her.

Sonia picks my kitty up, all brown and slimy in her arms. "Mote Thote dirty," she says. "I go wash her clean." And I hear her—the only one of Everybody Here who even does.

I smile at my friend and tell her, "Thank you!"

After about a million years, we get all the mud and dirt and ants cleaned up. Everybody Here helps out, once they finish screaming—everybody but cept Sonia, who gots Motorthroat, and Justin Ryan, who just sleeps. Daddy finds some new dry dirt to fill with all the ants. Then he sticks the farm upstairs in Alan's room, where Motorthroat can't go.

"Where is That Darn Cat?" Mommy asks suddenly.

"She's with Sonia," I answer her, feeling sparkly once again. "Sonia's washing her."

"What?" Mommy does not look sparkly. Milk swims over her face, and her eyes turn wet with worried. She scrambles up from the rug, where she was busy smearing Calamine on Alan's ant bites. She runs hard-breathing quick upstairs into the bathroom. "Where's she doing it?" she asks, bouncing back downstairs alone.

"In the kitchen, Mommy." I jump up to show her, but Mommy gets there first.

"Where's the kitty, Sonia?" I hear her ask tween breathing even harder.

"In washer," Sonia says. "I wash kitty clean."

And Mommy screams again.

This scream sounds different from the one for seeing mud and dirt and ants spilling all across her rug. I race to where she's kneeling front the washer, but Mommy blocks my seeing with her body. "Go back to the living room, honey," she orders me, in a voice all mixed with wild wind.

But I peek anyways.

And I see my kitty Motorthroat.

I see her tween Mommy's stretched-out arms, past Sonia's sunrise smile. I see her inside the clear round circle door sticked on the washer.

And Motorthroat is clean.

But my brain feels very dirty, and I don't think I will feel sparkly again till past forever.

22.

DIRTY

Still, my brain feels dirty.

Days and weeks have walked on by—only years can roll like wheels—and school with Mrs. Stone after New Year's starts without me. School with Mrs. Stone means school with Sonia too, and I never want to see her anymore.

I *hate* that dumb old Sonia!

I want to stick *her* inside our washer, spin her round in circles.

I want to wash *her* clean, the same way she washed Motorthroat.

But thinking about this doesn't make my brain feel clean at all. Instead, my brain feels stuffed with dirt and ants and worms and snakes. Not Alan's dirt or ants or worms or snakes, but scary ones that bite my brain whenever I fall asleep.

Every night I wake up screaming.

Every day I just sit in our house and do not play. I don't write any stories in the notebooks Sonia gave me. I don't draw any pictures of Martians with ten red eyes. I just tear out those empty pages and throw them all away—like the washer tore up Motorthroat, so Daddy had to throw her away too.

He didn't really throw her away, of course. Not into the garbage can with eggshells and potato peelings, or even into the wastebasket with papers crumpled into snowballs. Instead, he sticked her in a shoebox. Then he buried her in our backyard, beneath the mud and snow.

He planted a cross on top for her, and we all sang a song from Sunday School. That is what is called a funeral. I felt better singing about my kitty up in Heaven. My brain made pictures of her up there eating mushrooms and tuna, with chocolate chip cookies for dessert. (I don't think God would ever make her eat His lettuce.) In my brain-pictures she got to play with ornaments that never break. And she got to play with kitties that never break too.

But Motorthroat *did* break. She broke like those three glassy ornaments she batted off our tree.

I saw her.

And still, I feel like breaking Sonia.

Violence is uncool. That's what Skip said, my kidney-garden teacher with songs that skipped from the piano neath his fingers. And Daddy would agree. And Mommy would agree. And Caitlin would say I'm silly, and Alan would tell me I'm not logical. *Sonia didn't kill her on purpose,* he would say.

Only Haley-paley would call her a Dummy Head. She'd clonk her on the nose for me if she was in third grade. But she isn't. Haley-paley's still a Kidney Garden Baby. I called her that on Christmas Day, cause I felt mad at even her.

I wanted to break up the whole world!

And I still do.

But wanting to break up the world makes my brain feel dirty.

How can I ever wash it clean again?

I try at first with soap and water, scrubbing all my hairs till fire springs up from the head-skin underneath. I try to cut beneath the skin with Mommy's sewing scissors, so's I can pour the soap and water inside my brain.

Then Mommy catches me, and she takes those scissors far away. But she doesn't spank me this time or even yell or scold. She only hugs me on her lap for about a million years. But I don't talk to her or even cry. I feel scared if my mouth opened, only dirt and ants and worms and snakes would come crawling out.

She and Daddy take me to a doctor, a smiley one who gives me games to play instead of shots. But I don't talk to her, and I don't play her games. Her playroom looks too clean for dirt and ants and worms and snakes.

What can wash my dirty gone?

I wonder about this one Sunday morning.

My teacher, Mrs. Davies, says it in our Memory Verse.

" 'Wash me, and I shall be whiter than snow.' " She explains the man who wrote that verse was asking God to wash him from his sins. How? I want to ask her. How could washing make him white like snow? And how could white snow take away the dirt inside his brain? But I don't ask her those questions. I keep my mouth shut tight there too, so dirt and ants and worms and snakes will not jump out from it.

Everybody every day tries to make me talk.

Mommy and Daddy try with hugs and comfort-words and stories.

Caitlin tries with promising to let me read one of her scary books about the future.

Mr. Emmett tries with his piano music, and Haley tries with her brand-new Cabbage Patch doll—which she's even named after me.

Mrs. Winthrop tries with her cookies and hot chocolate, plus with her animals made from shiny stuff that breaks.

Peter tries with Dileth and his new white rat named Vector. And Alan tries with his lizards and frogs and guinea pigs and snakes and worms and fruit flies. He even tries with the ants inside his farm from Sonia. But I scream again when Alan brings those out.

And when Sonia tries, I scream hardest of all.

She plogs into our house hooked around her mommy's waist, in a hug so huge the mommy almost cannot walk. Mrs. Gray looks tiny like a dried-up crunchy leaf, but she's pink instead of red cause she got better from the flu. Her hands clutch a small white box with holes punched in the lid. She says, "Sonia has something to tell you, honey."

Sonia tells it to her feets in her mumble-voice. "I sorry, Peggy. Sonia not mean to hurt Mote Thote." She keeps hugging her mommy stead of me. But I feel glad about this, cause no way would I ever hug that Sonia anymore. And no way would I answer her too.

Instead her mommy talks, watching me with rainy eyes. "We have another present for you, Peggy. She's not your kitty, I'm afraid, but we do hope she'll make up for it." And Sonia's mommy pulls the hole-punched lid off her white box.

Inside the box is curled a tiny marshmallow like Dileth. But instead of mousy ears like Dileth's and an earthworm tail, she gots pointy kitty ears and a fluffy Motorthroat tail. "Mew!" she says, instead of squeaking. Her eyes are not red dots, but slanty blue swimming pools filled with wavy clouds. All the rest of her looks white— white as the snow that maybe could wash the dirt clean from my brain.

"Oh, isn't she adorable!" Caitlin says that, never me. Her hands instead of mine scoop the furry marshmallow out the box and up against her chest.

"Cool!" Alan says that, never me. "Is she an albino? I know her eyes aren't pink, but could she be a partial albino anyways?"

"Oh, how thoughtful of you!" Mommy says that, never me. The TV volume lowers on her voice. "We'll all help Pegasus take care of her, of course. But we still might need to give her some time."

They all give me some time. They all stand huddled tight round Sonia and her mommy, round their whiter-than-snow kitty who will never-never be my Motorthroat. They all notice her instead of me.

But I don't care—cause this gives me time to sneak away.

I slink off upstairs to my room. Pull on my puffy coat, zip it up all by myself without the zipper sticking. Push my feets down into boots and hide my hands inside fat mittens. But I don't run back downstairs to ask Mommy can I go play outside in the snow. Instead, I shove my window up and slip through, no one knowing. I grab the outside tree and shiver down it, turning me into a lion so's my head will not feel dizzy.

I land safe in the snow, and the dizzy doesn't come. But inside me my brain still feels all dirty. How can I wash the inside-me with sparkly snow?

I roll and roll and roll in it, but that doesn't help. Sonia's snowy kitty keeps mewing in front my inside eyes. She keeps turning into Motorthroat, rolling and rolling and rolling inside the washer. When she does this, I start screaming.

But then Sonia rolls around inside the washer instead, and I feel happy. Not nice-happy like giving her a present, but mean-happy like shaking sticks or throwing bugs at her. Kind of like how I think Mitchell Brannon used to feel when he chased us.

This happy is a fat balloon that pops and turns all saggy. The saggy bits stay inside me afterwards, clogging up my brain and the hollow place just above my tummy.

I plog and plog through the endless snow. I stuff some beneath the hood of my puffy coat, but it only makes my outside-head feel splashed with icy water. My inside-head feels dirty like before. And when I stuff more snow inside the front of my coat, it only melts into water on the outside-skin above my tummy. It doesn't wash the hollow place inside me.

Who can do that for me?

And, all at once, I remember.

I wish I could go to Him being Baby Jesus, cause then He'd be smiling at me for sure. But the Baby Jesus lives inside our house, where Sonia is right now. Where Everybody Else stands round her, wanting me to stay her friend and keep her kitty-who's-not-Motorthroat. I don't *want* to do those things!

Besides, I remember the Baby didn't die yet to wash away my sins. Only the Man did that. The Man whose beard might scratch me if I climb on top His lap, His eyes burning straight into my hollow place.

Would His eyes look burny now instead of sparkly? Would He wear His grassy smile or a needle for His mouth? Would I dare now to climb on top His lap? And would I dare talk to even Him? How would He feel if I told Him about Sonia? What would He say if I told Him I no longer want her for my friend?

Mrs. Davies at Sunday School always says He wants us to love our enemies. To forgive our friends when they do wrong—just like He forgave the peoples who sticked Him to that cross. But what if I don't want to do that? Would Jesus still forgive me? Would He still wash the dirty from my brain?

There is only one way to find out.

I got to head on over to our church and visit Him, in His picture on the wall of my Sunday School class. Just like me and Haley did during the Christmas pageant. But cept this time I will go alone, all by myself, and walk instead of riding in the car.

How to find our church? It lives miles and miles away, across three big streets like the tongues of three giant dogs licking up millions of car-bones. I will be a walking people licked up by those tongues, not a car. Plus, there will be no grown-up hands hooked to mine to help me cross those streets.

But I still got to go to that church anyways. I'll need to ask directions how to get there, even though I didn't say one word to anybody for days and days and days. And even though I'm not allowed to talk to strangers. But a stranger wouldn't act surprised, cause he wouldn't know that I no longer talk. And a grown-up stranger, or maybe even a big-kid one, might know where lives my white and woody church.

So on I plog through the snow, looking for peoples outlined black against it stead of twisty trees. I no longer care if those peoples might be strangers. And I no longer care that I have to cross big streets all by myself, even though I'm not allowed to do that either. My brain is already slimed with dirt and ants and worms and snakes. A few more dirty things will not make it any difference.

The important thing is washing it all clean. . . .

There. A tall black tree is plogging toward me through the snow. This tree gots people-type arms and legs and head, so I know it is actually a much-bigger human being. "Excuse me," I say to him in my politest grown-up voice. "Could you please tell me where I might find—"

The people-tree pushes me over.

He pushes hard against my front, knocking me down in the snow before I even finish up my question. He shuts that question off like water from a faucet, twisting tight my neck to "off" with his giant hands. Then he climbs on top me, breathing sour stink into my face.

The stink comes from not his mouth, cause he gots no mouth. His face is only clothy black with two big holes for eyes. He looks like Mr. Stranger Danger, in the color books we got from that policeman in third grade. But cept this people-tree is not a stranger.

I know that, soon's he starts to talk.

"So, you little turkey. You out here all alone? No big sis holding your hand? No big four-eyed Superdork flyin' in to rescue you with his big bad little mousie?"

Hairy Barry!

I do not answer him. His fingers still squeeze gone all my talking. Besides, I feel much too freezed inside. Hairy Barry's eyes are chunks of ice, stabbing me like points through the holes of his faceless face. He's all big and snarly and scary, like the monsters neath my bed, like a black cloud throwing lightning forks before a thunderstorm.

He looks a zillion times meaner than Mr. Stranger Danger. He also looks meaner than Mitchell Brannon ever did—even with his globs of mud before he became Alan's friend stead of his enemy. This boy used to be Caitlin's friend, but now he is *her* enemy. And Peter's too. And even mine.

Plus, he is right.

I *am* out here all alone, without Caitlin or Peter or even Alan to protect me.

Who will save me from Hairy Barry?

23.

GETTING SAVED TWO WAYS

First, I try to call the lion inside me.

"Grrrr!" She roars in her best scary-lion voice. But her roar gets squeezed gone like faucet-water, cause my throat is still twisted to "off" by Hairy Barry's fingers.

I try to turn my own fingers into her pointy claws. But the claws stay hiding scared inside my fat and snow-sogged mittens. Plus the mittens bat just air, cause Hairy Barry keeps his monster body out of reach.

I try to make my own teeth grow sharp points on their ends. But those teeth just stay square-shaped, like ice cubes stead of icicles. They shiver against each other, making clicks like buttons pushed on Alan's new computer.

And Hairy Barry only laughs.

This laugh makes big snakes of ice slither down my back. It's the snarly, pointy-knife laugh of an Enemy. It sprays more sour stink from the mouth behind his mask, and I magine that mouth's also filled with a million giant teeth. And not lion teeth, either.

Sharky teeth.

Teeth sharp as the realife knife that right now flashes up from inside one of Barry's stony fists—

I need a lion *outside* me!

And, all at once, I remember how to find one.

Jesus is a Lion! Mrs. Davies at Sunday School said He is the Lion of the Tribe of Judah. She also said He is a Lamb. That sounded silly to me when I first heard it, like when she told us He is both God and God's Son at the same time. But then she explained us how God can do everything. And how He was a Lamb when He died on the cross to save us from our sins.

Will He now be a Lion and save me from Hairy Barry?

I have to find out—before that pointy knife flashes any closer to me.

Pointy knives can kill people. So can pointy nails, like the kind those bad men used to fasten Jesus to that cross. They killed Jesus. Nobody saved Him—not even God who was His Father. Just like nobody saved Motorthroat from spinning inside the washer. God let her die too. Maybe He will also let me die from Barry's knife—specially since I wished inside me Sonia would die.

Jesus didn't wish that. The peoples who killed Him were even worse than Sonia, cause they killed Him on purpose. They were sharky-mean like Hairy Barry, not just slow and not-knowing like Sonia. But He didn't hate them anyways. He didn't kill them back or even wish them dead. Instead He said, "Father, forgive them, for they don't know what they do."

Sonia didn't know what she was doing. She wanted to clean Motorthroat, wash the mud off her. Not hurt her or kill her. And even if she did kill her, she didn't kill me. She was still my best friend. That means if I hate her now, I am very bad. Even if I do go to Heaven when I die, cause Mommy and Daddy say little kids get to go there anyways. If Jesus lets me die right this second, I still deserve to.

Besides, He isn't even here. He is miles away at church inside my Sunday School class, sticked up on the wall inside that picture....

Or is He?

Didn't Mrs. Davies say God is everywhere? And if God is also Jesus, then Jesus is everywhere too. Alan would say that is only logical. It also means Jesus *is* here, after all. I can call for help from Him right now. I can ask Him to save me—from both my sins, cause they're the dirt inside my brain, *and* from that sharky Hairy Barry.

So I do.

I ask Him as the Lamb to save me from my sins, and then I ask Him as the Lion to save me from Hairy Barry. I ask Him not with yelling but with my inside-talking, cause my throat still feels too choky from Hairy Barry's fingers. But just then those fingers go all loose anyways, and something peels them right off my neck.

They go loose, get peeled off my neck, right when I hear the Lion roaring.

"GRRRRRR!"

He is here!

He is the Lion *outside* me. The Lion of the Tribe of Judah. And He scares that old Hairy Barry something super silly.

Barry let go me fast and hops up like a frog. And the knife inside his stony hand slips out and bounces down into the snow. His eyes inside their holes grow big as the holes themselves. The rest of his face is still black cloth, but I magine that behind his mask scared milk is swimming across his skin. And I magine that his sharky smile has turned into a toothless little circle.

Hairy Barry starts walking backwards.

He keeps on walking backwards, his two giant palms facing out—until he lands smack into the arms of the policeman. The blue coated, red-faced policeman who just sneaked up behind him.

The policeman clicks two silver circles round his wrists, hooked together with a little chain. He pats him up and down all over, then says lots of words to him from a paper. Then Everybody Else swarms round *me* in a circle. Mommy and Daddy. Alan and Caitlin. Mrs. Gray and Sonia.

They all catch me inside a million toast-warm hugs. Nobody spanks or scolds me for sneaking out the house.

Mommy cries instead of yelling. Sonia's mommy also cries, but Sonia smiles at me like a sunrise.

This time, I smile right back at her. I hug her right back too when she wraps her arms round me. "You're my best friend, Sonia," I tell her through my hug.

And that is when I feel my brain washed clean, whiter than snow.

I feel sparkly inside once again.

And I know the Lamb has also come and washed away my sins.

"Man, that was really cool!" Alan tells me as we plog back to our car. "Did you see what happened, who saved your life back there?"

"Yes! It was Jesus, who is also God. Alan, you know what? He saved me in two different ways. The Lamb inside me saved me from the dirt inside my brain, and the Lion *outside* me saved me from that sharky Hairy Barry."

Alan stares at me with unfixed puzzles in his eyes, like I said something Not Logical. "What're you talking about, Pegasus? I didn't see any lambs or lions. The person who saved you was actually Sonia!"

"What?" I stare back at him for about a million years, my smile turning into a giant circle. "What do you mean, Alan? How could Sonia save me from my sins or Hairy Barry?"

"Well, I don't think she could save you from your sins. But man, she sure saved you from that gross Barry Bruner! He about had a cow when she showed up roaring at him. I think she actually scares him, Pegasus. Remember when he ran away from her that day at the Science Fair?"

I wrinkle up my nose, remembering. "He didn't run from Sonia, Alan. He ran from Luke and Leia and Kermit and Fang and Dileth. He is scared of . . ." I stop and think a minute for the names Alan calls them. " . . . reptiles and amphibians and small mammals. Sonia is a big mammal, 'cause she's a human being same as us. Why would he be scared of her?"

"It's 'cause she's different, Pegasus. I think Barry Bruner is scared of anybody who is different."

"That's not logical, Alan. We are different too, and he's not scared of us. Besides, Daddy says God made everybody different."

"True, but He made some of us more different than others."

I stop arguing then for the rest of our ride home. Too many other peoples are talking all at once. Their talking mixes up lions and birds, angry and happy at the same time. They sound angry about what mean old Barry tried to do to me, but happy I got saved from him. Plus, cause I am talking again the way I used to. Everybody asks me about a million questions, I think maybe just to hear me talking.

At my house I run back upstairs to my room. Mommy tries to follow me, but Daddy puts his "stop" hand on her arm. "Let's give her a little time," he says. I do need a little time, but not this time to sneak out my window into snow. I just want some time to think about what Alan told me.

No Lambs or Lions came to rescue me?

My rescuer was only Sonia?

Does that mean Jesus *didn't* come and save me, after all?

Thinking about this makes the sparkly in me fade to cloudy. I wonder, just a little bit, if He might still be mad at me. But that is not logical, cause I no longer hate Sonia. I no longer wish to see her spinned around inside our washer. Instead, I love my friend for saving my life. I love her cause she did just what Jesus said to do. And all that love inside me washed my brain whiter than snow....

"Mew!" Someone soft and tickly pushes herself beneath my hands.

I scoop her up and press her purring warm against my chest. She purrs just like Motorthroat, even though her bony, squiggly body is much smaller. Motorthroat felt huge and quiet like a furry pillow, and Mommy said she was a grown-up lady. But this new kitty is still a little girl. I think if she was human, she would be exactly my-sized. She fits perfectly inside my arms. And I no longer hate her for not being Motorthroat.

"Your name is Snow," I tell her now. "That's 'cause your fur is whiter than snow, just like inside me with the dirt all washed away. And your eyes look like snow too, all sparkly just the way I feel inside again."

And I do. Because right then I realize something.

"Mommy, Daddy, Caitlin, Alan!" I race out my room and back downstairs with Snow inside my arms. "You know what? Jesus saved my life today! He saved me in two different ways, from both my sins and Hairy Barry. He saved me by sending Sonia to come an' rescue me—just like He gave Haley her Cabbage Patch doll by sending Sandy Claws to bring her."

Mommy and Caitlin roll their eyes when I say that. I start to explain to them I know Sandy Claws is just pretend, but he still makes a good what Daddy calls *analogy*. But when Daddy wraps his arms round me and hugs me with his eyes, my mommy and big sister join right in with him.

Alan doesn't hug me, but he glows at me with his biggest leafy smile. "That is logical, Pegasus," he tells me, reaching out to scratch behind Snow's ears. "Do you think it's also logical this kitten is a partial albino?"

"Mew!" Snow answers him. But none of us can tell if that means yes or no.

24.

TWO BIRTHDAY PARTIES

"Oh, dear, Margaret! That sounds terrible."

My Sunday School teacher, Mrs. Davies, is looking slightly green. Lots of grown-ups do when I tell them my story—specially the part about how Motorthroat got spinned all flat and dead inside the washer. And the part where Hairy Barry strangled me with his knife sticked in my face.

"Does anyone else want to share what happened over Christmas vacation?" Mrs. Davies zips her face real fast around the room, her voice and eyes all trembly. But nobody answers her, cause they're all too busy watching me with interested.

So I raise my hand again, even though I'm not Anyone Else. "Wait, it gots a happy ending," I say quick with a smile, before she can even call on me. "See, I got washed clean just like Motorthroat. But 'cept I didn't die like Motorthroat inside the washer. When the Lamb of God washed all the dirt and ants and worms and snakes out from my brain, I came out still alive—"

Mrs. Davies interrupts by telling us it's time to say our Memory Verse. I don't scold her for interrupting, even though Mommy always tells us that is rude. I remember most ladies don't like hearing about those worms and snakes.

But after church, right when we are eating Sunday dinner, the phone chirps and it's her husband Pastor Davies. He tells Daddy he would like to meet us in his office, so's I can tell my story to him.

Well, I feel a million worms and snakes go slithering through my tummy, cause I wonder is he mad at me for scaring Mrs. Davies with all those worms and snakes. But that afternoon, when I sit with Mommy and Daddy in his church office of books and plants and rug like calm blue ocean, Pastor Davies only smiles when I tell my story.

And then he says, "Young lady, it sounds to me like you've been Born Again."

"What means 'Borned Again'?" I ask, so he explains by reading from the book God wrote us called the Bible.

"Honey, are you sure you understand?" Mommy asks when he is done, sounding worried. I know this is cause the Bible talks in funny words, and Mommy thinks I am too little to make sense of them.

I don't like her thinking I'm too little. So I sit up straight in my puffy chair that almost swallows me whole (it looks like a gray whale leaping from the rug-ocean), and I try real hard to change those funny words into regular ones. And when I do this, I can get their meanings—specially when Pastor Davies explains me them some more.

"Did we understand all that?" Daddy asks me this time.

"I did," I tell him. "Did you and Mommy understand it?"

"I don't know, baby. You tell us." He smiles all crinkly-eyed at me, and so I do.

"It means I died too," I explain. "Just like Jesus on the cross and Motorthroat in the washer. But 'cept it wasn't my outside-self who died, like with Motorthroat or Jesus. Instead it was my inside-self, the old Pegasus, who really hated Sonia 'cause I had lots of dirt and ants and worms and snakes of hate inside my brain." I stop to check on Mommy, but she doesn't look too green or trembly yet so I go on.

TWO BIRTHDAY PARTIES 167

"But when I called on the Lamb of God to save me, and He washed my brain all clean so's I could forgive Sonia, I came right back to life again—just like He did when He walked out from that cave they sticked Him in after He died.

"And the new Pegasus, my inside-self who came alive again, was the one who felt all clean and sparkly from forgiving Sonia. I could do that, Pastor Davies said, 'cause Jesus forgave me. And Him forgiving me is what made me come alive. And *that's* what Pastor Davies calls being Borned Again."

The grown-ups all stare at me like I just sprouted realife wings out from my back. Then they're all hugging me and telling me I'm smart, till I think they might swallow me more than that squishy chair-whale. But at last they all grow quiet, and Pastor Davies talks to me some more.

He explains me that my inside-self is a newborn baby, littler even than Haley's brother Justin Ryan. And cause that inside-self got Borned Again, she gets to have a birthday party. Not one like the birthday parties for my outside-self, with presents and balloons and chocolate cake with pink candles sticked on top. The party for my inside-self is the kind he calls Get Baptized.

"Would you like to do that, young lady?"

I think about this. "You mean this year I can have *two* birthday parties?"

"Yes," Pastor Davies answers, so I say that back to him. And I feel extra sparkly inside when everybody laughs.

Get Baptized feels sort of like a swimming party. There's a little swimming pool in church that's called a baptistry, only you can't usually swim in it or splash or dive or float on duck-faced rafts. And to step inside that swimming pool, you don't wear a swimsuit with orange suns on it smiling neath black glasses. Instead, you wear a snowy nightgown with no pictures on at all.

I like that funny nightgown, though. It looks all clean and sparkly, the same way my whiter-than-snow self feels inside. And I like stepping down into the swimming pool, cause the water in there feels all warm and hugging like bathtub water. I even like answering the questions Pastor Davies asks me in the swimming pool. He smiles and nods when I answer, so I think I got them all correct.

But I *don't* like the thing he does next.

Pastor Davies tells me plug my nose with both my hands. He explained me before what would happen to me then, but he never explained me how it would *feel*. So when he turns one hand into a cup and slides it round my head, then presses his other hand flat against my back, I still have no idea what is coming. And when I whoosh on backwards underneath that glugging water, it feels like fishies getting trapped inside my choking nose-holes.

Will those fishies made from water make my outside-self die too?

I don't know for sure. But I feel scared enough to chase them gone by turning into a whale—an even bigger whale than that chair inside Pastor Davies' office.

My flapping whale flippers splash a whole ocean of water outside that swimming pool. My plugged-up nose-holes cough the fishies out in two big rivers, and my choking throat coughs out a giant scream. And afterwards, my nose-holes feel all burny inside. Plus, my eyes rain down big salty tears that mix up with the water.

"She was just too little," Caitlin complains, when everybody but cept her hugs me with warm hands and eyes and towels. Daddy glares at Pastor Davies like he wants to punch his nose, and tomato juice swims over

TWO BIRTHDAY PARTIES

both their faces. I think that color means mad for Daddy, but only embarrassed for Pastor Davies. When he hugs me, he tells me he is sorry.

Tomato juice also swims over Caitlin's face, and she glares at me with both mad *and* embarrassed. "I don't think she even knew what was going on," she complains to Mommy and Daddy. "How on earth can a five-year-old understand religion?"

"A five-and-a-half-year-old," I correct her. "That is just my outside-self's age anyways. My inside-self is actually only one week old. She doesn't understand religion, whatever that thing is. But she does understand what was going on tonight. She knows Jesus washed gone all the hate things from her old self and made her brand-new inside-self come alive."

Caitlin stares at me real surprised. Daddy hugs me once more with his smile, then turns his smile on Caitlin. "There, honey, does that answer your question? I think our Pegasus can understand these things even better than we can, because she has the faith of a little child."

"But 'cept when I think my outside-self will die beneath the water," I remind him. "Then I have the scaredness of a whale!"

Daddy laughs this time. He scoops me high inside his orange lion-haired arms, and my nose-holes no longer feel burny.

My second birthday party doesn't happen till the summer.

This one seems not so interesting at first. That is cause it's much more like the ones I had other years, with presents and balloons and chocolate cake with pink candles sticked on top. But cept this is the first year I get six of those candles.

Like always, I blow on them and make a secret wish. And like always I blow spit that makes the fires only dance, so Haley has to poof them gone for me with her own wind. That is one more thing she can do better than me. But I feel much too sparkly inside for being jealous.

Everything else at my party is lots of fun. And not just all those fun things we usually do either, like making pudding from cake and ice cream all mushed up together or playing Pin the Tail on the Donkey. (This year my friend Ashley pins the tail to *Haley's* bottom. But last year Haley-paley did the same thing to me, so that's really not so unusual.) The things we *don't* do usually are even more fun. And they are also much more interesting.

One of these is Sonia playing the piano.

She plays, for Musical Chairs, my two favorite green-and-yellow songs. One of those songs is filled with sunshine, prancing like many golden stripes through shaggy grasses. In the other song that sunshine peeks through lots of sparkly diamonds, made by raindrops trapped inside the holes of spiderwebs. Mr. Emmett says those songs were written by a man named Mozart, who could already write songs when he was only three.

Could Sonia play piano when she was only three? I wonder this when everybody claps and cheers for her. But I don't feel jealous of Sonia either. I only feel real happy my friends are clapping and cheering for her instead of teasing.

The other interesting thing is that this year my birthday wish actually comes true. This happens even though Haley and not me blew out my candles. After we eat the pudding made from mushed-up cake and ice cream (everyone eats this but cept Justin Ryan, who uses his to wash his hair), Daddy brings out and gives to me my secret wish.

"A Horse With Wings!" I yell, after tearing off the unicorn-painted paper. "By Margaret Elizabeth Kendall . . .

TWO BIRTHDAY PARTIES 171

Wait, Daddy. That's my realife name. Was this book actually written by *me?*"

"You should know," Alan says, and everybody laughs. And I laugh right along with them, specially when Daddy wraps me up inside his biggest lion-hug.

"I showed your book to my publisher, and he said literary talent must run rampant in our family," he explains me, smiling proudly. Mommy and Caitlin roll their eyes at him. But when he makes everyone turn quiet so's I can read to them, both Caitlin and Mommy start smiling just as big.

I read to them all afternoon, the stories of my life. Every time I finish a chapter, somebody else wants me to start in with the next one. Everyone at that party lives inside my book. So Peter and Mrs. Winthrop and Haley and her mommy and Mr. Emmett and Mrs. Gray and Sonia and all my other friends, plus all the peoples who live inside my family, all want me to keep on reading. And even Snow, my kitty, likes batting round my present's ripped-off paper painted with unicorns.

Afterwards everyone claps and cheers for me, same as they do for Sonia whenever she plays piano. Even Haley-paley claps for me. And peering tween her glowing mommy and her just-as-glowing Mr. Emmett, she looks happy for me instead of jealous.

That's the interesting thing at this party I like best.

25.

STILL GOOD FRIENDS

"Pegasus, how would you like to go to a new school?"

"Don't be silly, Mommy." I laugh to chase the snakes gone from my tummy while I swing. "Now is still the long hot sticky summer."

"I know, baby. I don't mean till September."

"You mean September in the fall? When the leaves turn crunchy again and painted bright with rainbow colors, and the air tastes full of smoke and crisp like apples?"

Mommy laughs when she tells me yes. "You're a born writer like your daddy, aren't you, baby? And that's exactly why we think the new school they just opened across town would be better for you. Better for Alan, too."

I slow my swing to stare at Mommy, puzzled. "But Alan's not a born writer. He's a born scientist and mathist."

"Mathematician," Mommy corrects me, laughing once again. "The new school will be great for kids like him too."

"Will it also be great for kids like Mitchell Brannon and Haley-paley?"

"Not exactly." Mommy shakes her head, looking worried. "You see, it's a school for gifted children."

I stop my swing with both feets in the dirt to think about this. "Aren't all children gifted?" I ask at last. "They all get gifts for Christmas and their birthdays, including Haley-paley and Mitchell. Why can't they go to the gifted school?"

Mommy laughs again. "This is a different kind of gifted," she explains. "It's a school for kids like Alan who could do algebra in first grade, and for kids like you who could read and write before they started kindergarten. And for kids who, also like you, could manage to catch up within a week of having missed over a month of school. Mrs. Stone could not believe your progress this year. She told me she thinks you need much more of a challenge."

"She said I *was* a challenge," I remind Mommy. "When I stayed home I forgot all my multiplication tables, and Alan had to tutor me to get those tables back inside my brain. Remember that?"

"But you relearned them all quickly, didn't you, honey? And you still could read and write well enough to tutor him." Mommy pulls on her thinking face. "Remember how in your old school you two always felt so different? How Alan got teased for studying bugs, and you for being the littlest girl in your class?"

I nod. The snakes and worms have slithered back into my tummy.

"Well, at your new school there'll be lots of kids who study bugs like Alan, and lots of kids in your class who are just your size. They'll like the same things you like, as well."

"But Mommy, they already do! Mitchell likes studying bugs now same as Alan, and Alan likes dropping stink bombs same as Mitchell. Plus, Ashley and Danielle like pretending same as me to be unicorns and flying horses. And even Haley-paley likes arguing same as me. She's my friend again too, and the other kids don't tease me or Alan anymore."

But then I remember someone else.

"Mommy, what about Sonia? The other kids still tease her sometimes. If we go to this new school, she'll be with them all alone. Who will be there to protect her?"

Mommy smiles at me and smoothes my hairs. "You don't need to worry about Sonia, Pegasus. She's going to high school with Caitlin in the fall. She'll be in a new special class for kids just like her, who are teenagers like her but do work she'll understand. And besides, do you know what?"

"What, Mommy?" A happy birdie flutters in my chest, cause I can tell from her face the news is good.

"Three afternoons a week, you'll see Sonia at your new school too! Mr. Emmett told me he's had her placed in their program for musically gifted children. She'll take lessons there from him in the advanced piano lab."

I clap my hands, feeling sparkly inside again. Sonia will be safe! Plus, I'll have one friend at my new school I already know.

"I like Mr. Emmett," I tell Mommy while I pump my legs out straight to swing some more. "You know why?" I just remembered something. "He *always* liked Sonia—even back before he knew how good she could play piano. So I'm glad he's her teacher. And I'm also glad he's going to be a new daddy for Haley and Justin Ryan."

"I'm glad too," Mommy tells me, smiling. "For them and also for their mother. This one's promised to take her legally, and he's not about to dump her. He's committed himself to her and to her kids for life."

What Mommy means, I know, is that Mr. Emmett plans to marry Haley's and Justin Ryan's mommy. Only next Saturday.

Mommy and Daddy and Caitlin and Alan and me all get to go and watch their wedding. So do Mrs. Winthrop and Mrs. Gray, Sonia's mommy. So does Mr. Emmett's mommy from Chicago, plus all of his piano students. Including, of course, Sonia herself.

That makes about a million peoples. So they hold their wedding not inside our church, which is full of stinky candles and woody benches and long red tongues of velvet rug. Instead they let it be outside, with sunshine stead of candles, with wood still on the trunks of trees, with human tongues made red from punch instead of velvet. But cept some grunting men push a big thing out the church, which is the giant brown piano.

Sonia sits at that piano. Her fingers flash across its teeth, making dancing songs jump out. The songs are filled with leaves and wind and sun and sparkly rain, with smoky woods and midnight moons and honey-sweet white flowers. Haley's mommy wears lots of those flowers in her hair. Mr. Emmett wears just one white flower on his midnight jacket, but he smiles big at his bride like a whole bright rainbow.

He holds her hands and doesn't once wash his own hands without soap. And he doesn't once say, *Oh dear, oh dear.* His voice does sound all trembly when he promises Haley's mommy to love her and stay with her all his life. But I think his trembles come from feeling happy inside instead of worried.

Even Haley looks happy. She doesn't scream this time or sock my tummy or yell *I hate you* or even go running off to our Sunday School class. She's much too busy plucking snowy flowers from her basket, sprinkling them down the grassy path where her mommy goes floating like a lacy-snowy cloud. But cept baby Justin Ryan heads down that path right behind her.

Justin Ryan doesn't float. He doesn't even walk, cause he's only eight months old now and that is still too little. Instead, he crawls. He wriggles out from Mrs. Winthrop's wobbly arms, slides off to the grass, then gallops down the path on his hands and knees. He picks up Haley's dropped flowers and stuffs them into his mouth like candies. Mrs. Winthrop jumps up from her chair and charges after him, scoops him up and sticks her hand inside his mouth. She screams when he throws up all those flowers on her dress.

I think that baby is the most interesting part about this wedding.

I giggle at Justin Ryan, but when I see Haley I start feeling sad. It's hard to watch her get to be the Flower Girl, while I have to sit still on a chair and just observe. I feel, for one second, that sharp bee-sting of jealous. I wish I could be a Flower Girl same as Haley, and wear a lacy dress that matches the snowy flowers spilling from my basket.

Instead, I clutch upon my lap only my shiny purse. It's the one that used to have three plastic daisies sticked in front, only last summer I tore those off to give to Mrs. Winthrop. Plus, I'm wearing a pink dress that only matches my skin—and it really itches my skin, too.

But when Daddy hugs me to him, I feel sparkly once again. I feel happy to have a daddy who will never run away. And I feel happy for Haley too, getting Mr. Emmett for her new adopted daddy. He too will never run away. Plus, even Haley-paley has decided she likes him.

I know, cause she tells me this right after the wedding.

"I'm glad Emmett's going to be my daddy now. He said he loves me and Justin Ryan just the same, and he'll never again leave me out of the Christmas pageant. And you know what else, Margaret-pargaret?"

"What, Haley-paley?"

"He's the one who got me my Cabbage Patch doll! The one I feed and wash and dress while Mommy feeds and washes and dresses Justin Ryan. I heard him one day talking 'bout it in the other room to Mommy."

"Justin Ryan talked about your Cabbage Patch doll?"

"No, silly! Justin Ryan can't talk yet, but 'cept to say 'Mommy' and 'beets' and 'turtle.' *Emmett* talked about it. He asked Mommy not to tell me he's the one who got her, 'cause he was scared I might not like him buying me a present. But 'cept I do. I like when *anyone* buys me a present. It doesn't got to be old Sandy Claws."

"So Sandy Claws didn't bring her, Haley-paley?"

" 'Course not, silly." Haley laughs and shakes her head at me. "He's only pretend, I've already known that for years. I just like to argue with you, Margaret-pargaret. But you know what?" Her voice turns into a soft wind. "I don't think Jesus is pretend anymore. When I prayed to Him for a daddy, He brought me Emmett. And I think He told Emmett to buy me my dolly, too."

Haley looks all sparkly when she tells me that. But she doesn't look too sparkly a week later, when I tell her about going to a new school next year.

"You don't want to go to that old place, Margaret-pargaret. That's the smart kids' school. It's the dumbest place to go to in the world."

"That's not logical, Haley-paley. It's a new place, not an old one. Plus, how could it be both a smart kids' school and the dumbest place to go at the same time?"

Haley rolls her eyes at me. "It just could, you dumb ol' Margaret! Don't you know anything? Brittany and Sarah say that's the school for nerds. If you go there you'll be a nerd, just like your dumb ol' boy-poy brother Alan."

"Alan is not a nerd," I argue, feeling crawly and roaring-mad inside at the same time. "And he is not dumb, either. He is gifted, same as me." But then I stop, cause I notice Haley's all rolled up into a snuffly ball. "What's wrong?" I ask instead, feeling worried for her now.

"What about me?" Haley yells through her snuffling. "I guess *I'm* not gifted, and you don't even care!

You'll go off to your dumb smart kids' school and not want to be my friend anymore. You'll think you're so cool 'cause you can do things better'n me, like read an' write an' draw an' say big words like 'logical.' "

"No, Haley-paley. I'll always be your friend, whether you're gifted or not. Besides, I think you *are* gifted. You're gifted at catching balls and climbing jungle gyms and coloring inside the lines. You're also gifted at cutting straight and making paper snowflakes that look fresh from the clouds instead of melted. Plus, you can even ride a real bike without those training wheels."

"You could too, Margaret-pargaret. C'mon, I'll teach you how." Haley unballs herself and wipes off her tear-snakes on her T-shirt. Her smile bursts through her wet face like sun from behind a storm.

"Okay, Haley-paley." I smile back at her. "And then I'll teach you how to write a story."

So she does and I do. Only I keep wobbling on her bike and tipping over sideways to the grass. And she writes just one sentence, in crookedy first-grade printing with all the words spelled wrong. It doesn't matter, though, cause we are still good friends.

26.

GROWING UP TWO WAYS

I am six years old now—six years and not six fingers. I now know what the difference is between them. A year is a time unit of 365 days, though my brain still sees a picture of it being a giant wheel. (That wheel looks like a Ferris wheel, spinning round and down then back up high again.) But I still like to pretend my fingers are worms, pink earthworms fastened to my hands.

I still got ten of those fingers, but now I can use them to count all the way up past one thousand. I flash them over and over, like a picture of one thousand fingers hiding inside my brain.

This is a trick Alan taught me. I can use it to count all the way up to 1984, which is this year. It's also the name of a scary book about this year that Caitlin's friend Rachel left here once. I'm happy in this year *my* only Big Brother is Alan. He is lots nicer than the Big Brother inside that book.

My fingers can do many things, stuff they couldn't do last year. They can tie my shoestrings into bows and color inside the lines. (Well, almost.) They can cut straight along the dotted lines of paper dolls, though they still make all my paper snowflakes look like they are melted. They can swing me on top the jungle gym so long's I stay a lion, and steer the handlebars of my bike without those training wheels.

They can even play piano now, making dancing songs jump out the teeth instead of noises. Of course, the songs I play are lots easier than the ones Mr. Emmett gives Sonia. The songs he gives *everyone* else are easier than the ones he gives Sonia.

Mr. Emmett no longer says, *Oh dear, oh dear* when we make mistakes. Not even to me, who makes the most mistakes. I think he feels too happy from getting to teach Sonia, who never makes mistakes at all. I also think he feels too happy from getting Haley's mommy for his wife. And I think he likes being the daddy of Haley and Justin Ryan. They don't scream so much when he's around. Maybe that's cause they like him, and maybe it's just cause they're growing up.

Haley can read and write real stories now. She can also draw real peoples, though she still won't try to draw peoples on other planets. She can play softball and soccer on real teams where they pick her first, and she never once drops the ball or trips over it backwards. She can also play piano with her new adopted daddy as her teacher—better than I can, though still not good as Sonia. And she can even cook eggs without breaking some on her kitchen floor.

Justin Ryan always breaks eggs on the kitchen floor, but he is also growing up. He can run on his hind feets now when Haley chases him for throwing eggs. He can say about a million words, including all the miles-long science names for dinosaurs. My brother Alan likes to teach him those.

When Mrs. Winthrop baby-sits him and changes his diaper (Justin Ryan's, I mean), he tells her all about T-Rexes. "They were carnivores," he explains her while she's wiping his bare bottom. "That means they ate meat. And Triceratops was an herbivore who ate vegetables, even though he had three scary horns. And Apatosaurus—"

"Goodness." Mrs. Winthrop interrupts, head-shaking and clicking her tongue. "In my day toddlers only knew about doggies and kitties. Sonny, if you're smart enough to know the names of all those dreadful prehistoric monsters, aren't you old enough to be potty-trained?"

"No," Justin Ryan answers her, wriggling and giggling. "Not till I'm three fingers old."

I think we all have different ways of growing up.

Alan's way is learning how to read harder books, cause he no longer sees letters and words turned round backwards. A tutor at our new school is helping him with that. Plus, three new friends in his fourth-grade class are helping him build a talking robot. On weekends, though, he still plays with Mitchell—same as I still play with Haley-paley. He's teaching Mitchell and his other friends the names of the bugs they stick inside their stink bombs.

Caitlin's way of growing up is cutting her hair in steps again and painting her eyeskins blue. She also gots a new boyfriend, a football boy named Eric. He is okay, not mean like Hairy Barry. But he's not quite so nice or interesting as Peter.

Peter's way of growing up is taller and with only lions in his voice—no more birds. Also, he's not sad about Caitlin's new boyfriend. This is cause he gots a new girlfriend. She is Caitlin's best friend Rachel, who likes to read and write science stories about the future. Sometimes, only sometimes, I wish Rachel could be my sister stead of Caitlin. But it doesn't really matter, cause Peter's still our friend. And last week he gave me and Alan two baby white rats. They look just like Dileth—cause *she* turned out to be their mommy.

Sonia's way of growing up is learning how to add and subtract and write whole Compositions, plus read books as hard as the ones Haley reads. She likes the kind called fairy tales, with princesses and princes.

So does her boyfriend Kevin, who's in her new special class at the high school. (I guess getting a boyfriend is another way Sonia's growing up.) I like Kevin, too—even though he doesn't play piano good like Sonia. His eyes are blue and slanty like my kitty Snow's, and he and Sonia both love to play pretend with me. They pretend to be the Prince and the Princess, and I am the pastor who gets to marry them.

I got two different ways of growing up.

The first way is for my outside-self, who is pushing up taller as she learns how to do more things. Things like riding the bus to my new school, where I'm only in first grade now with lots of my-sized kids. But I don't feel sad about this, cause my new class is very interesting. We're reading whole chapter books, like the ones I read in third grade only harder. And we're writing real stories and poems and plays.

Last week we acted out a play I wrote all by myself. In it I got to be Pegasus, the realife horse with wings. My brand-new friends not in the play all clapped and cheered for me up there on stage. And, best of all, they also clapped and cheered for Sonia—cause she's the one who crashed out the music for our play on her piano.

I think when it comes to playing piano, Sonia has *already* grown up.

My second way of growing up is for my inside-self.

That self is still a baby, only one year old now stead of six. But she doesn't have to wear diapers or drink milk from her mommy like Justin Ryan did. She drinks milk instead from the book God wrote us called the Bible. This milk is made from words, only regular not funny ones like those in Pastor Davies' Bible. The Bible Daddy gave me gots words same as the ones we talk. He explained me if I read those words every day, my inside-self will grow bigger too.

Reading my Bible sometimes feels like working a hard puzzle. There are lots of little numbers with words sticked behind them, and you can find the words by looking up the numbers. At the back are lists of words with numbers next to them, and sometimes I will pick a word out from that list and then find from its number other words telling its meaning.

One day the word I pick is *pray.*

I pick that word cause of what happened the night before, when I waked up screaming again from a scary dream. The dream was about Hairy Barry and his knife and choking fingers. I waked up from it before Jesus could send Sonia to rescue me, so Mommy and Daddy came and rescued me instead. They took turns holding me and rocking me on their warm laps, and then they also prayed for me. God answered them by hugging me warm with a blanket I couldn't see.

Pray is a funny Sunday word. It means talk to God. Before last winter when Hairy Barry scared me in the snow, I never really talked to God. I thought *pray* meant to say those little poems Mommy taught me, folding my hands before supper or kneeling beside my bed at night. Maybe God liked to hear those poems, but I didn't think He'd ever answer them.

But after the day God rescued me, I found out I could talk to Him in real words, not just poems. So did Mommy and Daddy, cause they talked to Him about me in real words every night—specially when I waked up screaming from those scary dreams. They called that praying too. So I know *pray* must have different meanings.

When I look it up in the list back of my Bible, the numbers there match the Bible ones sticked to this sentence: *Love your enemies; pray for those who persecute you.* I know what is an *enemy* but not a *persecute.* So I look up its words and numbers too, and I learn it means to hurt someone.

Hairy Barry wanted to hurt me last Christmas in the snow. Does that mean he is my enemy? And when he pushed me down and sat on me and squeezed my throat and scared me with his knife, wasn't he persecuting me? If he was, then that logically means only one thing.

I got to both love and pray for him.

"Oh, honey." Mommy shakes her head when I ask her about this. "You don't need to think about that monster anymore. He's locked away in Juvenile Hall where he belongs." Her eyes flash with angry and sad at the same time. "It's just what he deserves too, for hurting my baby."

"I was not hurt, and I am not a baby," I tell her. "Besides, doesn't the Bible say we all deserve bad things? And didn't Jesus say we should forgive anyways, just like He forgave us anyways?"

Mommy shakes her head again, a mist swimming in her eyes. "Pegasus . . . " She stops and squeezes me real tight. "I don't deserve you, honey," she says, more softly this time. "Sometimes I think you teach me more than I could ever teach you."

"You mean about Mars and Pluto peoples and things I make up inside my head?"

"Well, those too." Mommy laughs when she lets me go. "But I mean more the kinds of real things you find inside your soul. Just don't go overboard, honey," she adds, looking again a little worried. "By all means go ahead and pray for that . . . boy." I know she says *boy* after choking *monster* back down her throat. "But I hope you keep on filling your head with Mars and Pluto peoples, too."

"Okay, Mommy." And I skip off to write a play about a Mars man who marries a Pluto lady.

But next bedtime, right after I say my always-poem to God, I also pray to Him about Hairy Barry. I tell God I forgive that boy, and I ask Him to wash all the dirt and ants and worms and snakes out from *his* brain. And that night inside my dream, when old Barry Bruner once again pushes me down into the snow and grabs my throat, I concentrate hard on loving him.

This time before I wake, Jesus comes and lifts gone Barry's fingers from my neck. But instead of washing gone *my* dirt and making *my* brain snow, He does this to the brain of Barry Bruner.

That night I wake up feeling sparkly, stead of screaming.

Sometimes I will still scream scared, and sometimes I'll feel sparkly. That's what Mommy and Daddy say my new life will be like. That's what Jesus said it will be like too in my Bible. But God can use anything to help me keep on growing up, including bad things.

My outside-self grows when I climb back on my wobbly bike and push forward with skinned-up knees (after they get Band-Aids on, of course). And my inside-self grows when I turn my bad-dream screaming into praying. God always answers me, hugging me warm inside His blanket of love I cannot see.

27.

PEGASUS WRITES HER PUBLISHER

Dear Mr. Publisher:
    I wish to say thank you for publishing my book *A Horse With Wings.*
    Thank you!
    There. I said it.
    I feel so sparkly inside to have my secret wish come true!
    Now to tell you all about some other things I wish. There are actually three wishes.
    Here is my first one. But first I got to tell you that enclosed are the last three chapters of *A Horse With Wings.* I couldn't stick those chapters in the copy you just published, cause back then I didn't write them yet. I finished them only today.
    Anyways. My first wish is this. Would you please add those last three chapters to your next printed copy of *A Horse With Wings?*
    Now to tell you the other things I wish. There are actually two more.
    And here is my second wish. If you do stick in those chapters, would you please mail one copy of *A Horse With Wings* free to Juvenile Hall for Barry Bruner? I would like him to read it so's he knows both God and me forgive him. And also cause it must feel *board*ing (that means even worse than boring) sitting in a place Mommy explained is a jail and a school at the same time.
    And here is my third wish. I can't love my enemy but cept in my screaming dreams. But we read about some peoples who can love him by going to visit him and tell him about God. They are called a Prison Ministry. So

would you please send some money that I get for my book to this Prison Ministry?

Well, those are all my wishes, so thank you very much.

Yours truly,
Margaret Elizabeth Kendall
(alias Pegasus, A Horse With Wings)

P.S. Oops! I forgot. There is one more wish. So I guess that actually makes four.

And here is my fourth wish. On the jacket of my last copy of *A Horse With Wings* (which gots no hood like my jacket but only two big sleeves with words on them), I drew my horse all sparkly-white like snow—even her wings. I like my horse looking snowy, cause that is how my inside-self feels washed clean from all its dirt and ants and worms and snakes.

But on the jacket of the next copy, would you please let me draw that horse so's her wings look different from her snowy body?

Daddy says all God's children are *unique* (a word I specially like, cause it sounds like *unicorn).* He borns us and makes us grow in many different patterns. So here is how I'd like to draw my horse's wings: soft as a wind, pink as fingers, and painted with lions and birds.

AUTHOR'S NOTE

This is a work of fiction. All characters and events in this novel are products of my imagination. Any direct resemblances to actual characters or events are strictly coincidental.

However, little Pegasus, the main character and narrator of this story, is in some respects a composite mix of myself and my two daughters as small children. She has the colorful imagination all three of us shared and, like my older daughter and myself, a sensitivity and empathy for people who are "different." She also has the feisty spirit of my younger daughter—who would defend larger children from bullies—as well as her spiritual precocity.

A Horse With Wings was also inspired by the novel *Buttons in the Back* by Elizabeth Kirtland (Vanguard Press, 1958), a delightful series of adventures narrated by another spirited small girl. I first read this novel back in 1983 and so set my novel in that year, intending at the time for it to be contemporary. Now I suppose it has a slightly historical feel (though not so much as that earlier narrative, which takes place back in 1916).

Oh, yes—as a child I really did once ask the question: "If your fingers had eyes and played the piano, wouldn't they get dizzy?" And I also really thought a certain Bible Memory Verse went: *I was glad when they said unto me, "Lettuce, go into the house of the Lord."*

p. 25 - his eyes (have)

p. 48 - full justify paragraph
p. 131 - extra blank page
(not needed)

Made in the USA
Charleston, SC
16 August 2010